The REBIRTH of MORGAN RANCH

a fiction story

by

Marsh Collins *and* Guy Lautard

Published by Makerworx, LLC

THE REBIRTH OF MORGAN RANCH. Copyright © 2022 by Marsh Collins and Guy Lautard.

Published by Makerworx, LLC, Ann Arbor, Michigan, USA.

1st printing, March 2022.

ISBN: 978-1-953439-01-7

Cover illustration:
Background photo by Alexis Mette via Unsplash, used under Unsplash License.
Murphy Rebel photo by Ken Hodge (Darwin, Australia), used under Creative Commons Attribution 2.0 Generic License.
Compositing by Daniel Grover.

Contents

This story was written by Marsh Collins and myself in about 2003. We each contributed to the plot and the contents, debated how some things should be worded, and generally had fun doing it. It's not put forward as great literature — it's simply a good story which we think you will enjoy. Marsh and I initially became friends due to his acquisition of (and contributions to) my Machinists' Bedside Reader books. I met Marsh and his wife Verna in 1997 on a trip to San Diego, and visited him again a few years later on a trip to Las Vegas and the Los Angeles Basin. We corresponded for many years on topics of mutual interest, and collaborated in writing "The Rebirth of Morgan Ranch" together. Sadly, Marsh passed away July 28, 2007.

Guy Lautard, Sechelt, B.C., March 2022

Chapter 1
Uninvited Guests

John laid the letter aside, gazing out the window across the snow-covered field, past the weathered barn, and on to the snowy ridge to the west. He could see the trace of the fire-road where it had all begun. It had originally been a logging road until the lease had been logged out to the permit's specifications, and then became simply a fire access road. The B.C. government only used it during Spring and Summer seasons to do maintenance to radio repeaters and weather facilities along the ridge — and for fire access if they ever had to fight a forest fire up there.

He knew the road was in bad shape. A heavy Fall rainstorm had washed major ruts into it at several points. Afterwards, the last government truck to try it, a 2½ ton 6x6, barely got through — and it took the winch to do it. The conifers obscured the trace much of the way, but the place where he had met the two of them was clearly visible.

He had been sitting right where he was now, idly watching the snow drifting down, waiting until the storm moved through before he would resume clearing the roads on the ranch in order to get feed out to his livestock. Suddenly he had noticed something out of the usual on the trace....

John went to the living room to get a pair of 16x70 Fujinon binoculars which he kept near the window. Through the binoculars he could see what looked like a Jeep or Land Cruiser, seemingly half-buried in snow.

Maybe I'd better go take a look-see, he had thought. Stretching as he rose, he'd shaken the kinks out of his lanky frame, shrugged into his parka and stuffed his feet into his insulated boots. In the barn he saddled Red, the big roan his uncle had raised from a headstrong colt to a spirited mountain-wise cattle horse. What a change this last year has been! he mused as he led Red out of the barn, mounted, and headed for the trail up the "short-cut."

John's Uncle Gilbert, his dad's older brother, had died of cancer a couple of years ago, leaving no direct heirs and no clear will. One consequence was that the ranch had gone on the block. John's dad, himself a retired semi-invalid, had backed John's bid, and, surprise of surprises, it was the winning — and only — offer. Times weren't all that good in the cattle business, and money was perennially short.

Now he was a cattle rancher, and learning new things every day. He had worked summers for his uncle during his high school years, so the routine was nothing new, but the out-of-the-ordinary things were enough to keep him on his toes. Like this idiot showing up on the fire access road in the middle of a snow storm!

The wind sliced deeply anywhere it could penetrate his parka. His gloves were stiff in the cold air. It had taken half an hour for him and Red to reach the trace. As he approached it, the vehicle resolved itself as a civilian Jeep with a hard-top and roll-bars. The problem was obvious: it had high-centered on a rock, tearing open the oil pan, judging from the black oil staining the snow downhill of it.

The passenger door opened and a boy of high-school age stepped out into the snow-drift and struggled toward John.

"I see you have a problem," John said by way of greeting. "You alone?"

"Nah, my mom is asleep. She's all wore out."

"What are you doing way up here in this weather? There's nothing up here that would interest anyone but the government or maybe the phone company."

"She got lost, I guess." The boy was surly, accusative.

"Well, what do you plan to do? Have you contacted anyone?" John asked, looking at the Jeep's CB antenna. Not much chance of raising anyone from here, particularly in this weather.

The drivers' side door opened against the wind and swirling snow. A woman wrapped in a heavy parka stumbled out and nearly fell. John dismounted, helped her regain her footing, and led her around to the lee of the Jeep.

"Thank you," she muttered, sounding disoriented. "I guess we got lost. We were looking for the Rodgers Ranch."

John studied her as she regained her composure.

"You're lost, all right. The Rodgers place is another ten miles up the highway, and then back several miles on a dirt road. They won't plow it until the storm quits, which won't be for another day or two."

He looked meaningfully toward the streak of black oil, soon to be covered by the falling snow.

"Looks like you have a serious problem. Have you anyone to call to get you into town?"

"No. The radio doesn't work, and no one knows where we went. I don't know what to do. I'm not acquainted with this kind of country."

Great! John thought to himself. A city woman, wandering around 75/80 miles from the closest town of any size, and gets herself lost on an abandoned logging trace!

The boy spoke up, "You're just dumb, Mom! Bringin' me out here an' gettin' lost! What'dya use fer brains?"

"Whoah, kid!" John cut him off sharply. "You haven't earned the right to criticize your mom! Not until you show what you can do yourself. I don't see you showing us any good solutions!" He glared at the smart-mouth, then glanced at the woman. She appeared — from what he could see of her — to be about mid-30's; a wisp of dark brown hair had escaped her parka. Her brown eyes had a tired, exasperated look, and she was obviously exhausted. A tear crept from the corner of one eye and rolled down her cheek. She wasn't going to be much help.

"I'm John Morgan. I live down there. This is actually part of my ranch. I'll go get my tractor, and pull your car down to the ranch house, and then we can figure what to do next. There's not much shelter on this horse, and he can't carry more than two. You don't want to try to walk out of here in this stuff. Are you OK to stay with the car until I get back — say a couple of hours?"

"Yes. It's cold, but I guess we'll be alright."

"Why'nt you take me with you? I don't need to stay here!" the kid whined.

"You're going to stay here and look out for your mother until I get back. Understand me?" John already had a bad taste in his mouth about this snot-nose. If you freeze before I get back, it won't be much of a loss, John thought to himself.

*   *   *

Five hours later the three of them ruefully surveyed the Jeep, which they had towed into the ranch's main yard.

The engine pan had a gash where the protective plate had been torn from the pan as it encountered the snow-covered rock. There was obviously no oil left, and the woman, running the engine to run the heater, had caused the engine to seize. There was major damage. John led them to the house, shaking his head.

4

It was late afternoon, and nothing more could be done until tomorrow. They shrugged out of their parkas, and John got his first good look at his uninvited guests. The kid was skin-and-bones, tow-head, with freckles and a pugnacious look. A smart-ass, John thought.

The woman was about 35, medium height and slender. Slightly swarthy skin, expressive large dark brown eyes and a straight, up-tilted nose gave her a piquant, almost pixie look. She was scared and confused about what to do now.

"I'm Lois Milner, and this is my son Peter. We were on our way to see my sister. Do you know Zeke Rodgers? He's my sister's husband. We've never been there before, and weren't expecting the weather to be so bad."

"Do you want to call Rodgers from here? Today's Thursday. It's going to take most of tomorrow to load your Jeep onto my flat-bed, get it into Kamloops, and get it into a shop for repair. There's no shop closer that can do the work your engine's going to need. Maybe Rodgers'll come down and get you."

John watched the uncertain light play in her eyes; she wasn't too enthusiastic about phoning Rodgers. John had never met the man, but had heard he was a hard type, to put it mildly.

"Well, I don't know if he would, but I'll try." There was heavy doubt in her voice. He gestured toward the phone and opened the book to the page where Warren Ezekiel Rodgers was listed.

The phone was in the ranch house living room, and even from the kitchen John could hear her side of the conversation.

"Ellen, I need Zeke to talk to Peter — to talk some sense into him. He's taken up with the Shugard boys again, and I have no control over him. He's in trouble with the law now, and I'm really afraid of what will come next."

There was a long pause, two or three minutes, then Lois spoke again.

"But why won't Zeke even talk to me? I'm at my wit's end! Peter's not bad. He just seems to gravitate to these dopers. I can't get him to listen to me at all."

Another pause and then she was describing their present situation.

"…and I know it'll be expensive to fix. I don't have anything like enough money to get it fixed. I don't know what I'm going to do!"

The rest of the conversation became lost to John as he began fixing some ground beef. Hamburgers would make a good dinner for three people who'd missed lunch during a strenuous day.

Lois appeared near tears when she came back to the kitchen.

"I don't know how I'm going to pay you for what you've done. I don't even know if I can afford to have my Jeep fixed." She was having trouble holding on to her composure.

"For now, don't worry about it. There's no charge for getting your car down off the mountain, nor for putting you and your boy up for a few days. As for the car, we'll take it into Kamloops tomorrow and see about what it'll take to fix it. Let's take things one step at a time."

He sliced some onions into the ground beef. "I gather your brother-in-law wasn't too receptive."

"You got that right! He said he was done talking to Peter. 'If he wants to be a jailbird, let him go to it,' was all he said — and not even to me, but through Ellie!" Tears of anger and frustration rolled down her cheeks.

Peter stormed into the kitchen.

"What's the matter with the stupid teevee?" he demanded. "There's nothin' on except some dumb egghead concert an' the news!"

"It's not the fault of the TV set. We only get two channels here. And I like it here." The last sentence was stated as harsh as the complaint had been delivered.

Peter lost his belligerence and shuffled back into the living room. Flopping into a chair, he picked up a magazine about home-built airplanes and started to thumb idly through it.

Lois had at first stiffened with resentment, but then realized that here was someone Peter was NOT going to bulldoze. She looked more closely at this rangy, straw-haired man as he set out an electric grill and began making beef patties while it heated. She applied herself to a fresh head of lettuce, peeling off enough for three hamburgers, and then began setting the table. John noticed this and grinned at her. This gal must have some spunk in her. At least she isn't going to roll up in a ball and cry the whole time.

The next day they hauled the Jeep into Kamloops. The news on the damage wasn't good. There was a lot to be done before it would be operational again. It was no news to John, as he had seen the external damage, and knew there was plenty inside.

On the drive back from Kamloops, John decided that both he and his guests could do with a little diversionary treat. Poor woman, he thought, she's had a hard couple of days. Maybe a little chocolate fudge will pick her up. I know it will me. If it were just the smart-mouth kid, he wouldn't bother. When John was out-of-sorts he would sometimes make something good to eat, something out of the ordinary. Tonight he was going to make some serious fudge.

When they got home, John again prepared dinner. Lois pitched in and set the table. Pete was sullen throughout the dinner, although John and Lois held a lively conversation, ignoring his sulk.

After the dinner dishes had been washed up and put away, his suggestion to Lois that they make chocolate fudge was met with enthusiasm, so he set his guest to greasing a 10" square glass baking pan with butter, while he went into the pantry to dig out the ingredients.

Assembling the needed ingredients on the kitchen table, he ticked them off in his mind in silence.

A 12 ounce can of unsweetened evaporated milk.
A canister of white sugar.
18 ounces of top quality semi-sweet baker's dark chocolate.
1/2 pound of butter.
8 ounces of marshmallows.
2 heaping tablespoons of vanilla.
2 cups of chopped walnuts.

Next, he set a thick-bottomed 6-quart saucepan on the stove and dug a wooden spoon out of a drawer. The electric mixer was always ready for business, with its beater waiting in the bowl. He checked again that everything he would need was ready, then washed the can of evaporated milk, punched two holes in the top, and poured the contents into the saucepan.

Next he poured white sugar into a smaller saucepan. Seeing no apparent attempt at measurement, Lois wondered out loud how he knew when he had the correct amount.

John shrugged. "Done it before. Lots of times, back when I was younger than Pete. And since. When it gets to about there it's enough — 4-1/2 cups. Actually, even half that amount of sugar is enough."

The sugar then went into the saucepan with the evaporated milk, after which John turned on the heat, and began to stir with the wooden spoon. When the mixture came to a full boil he turned the heat down quite a ways, glanced at his watch, and continued to stir.

"I gotta keep stirring this stuff non-stop for about 20 minutes. Would you mind unwrapping the butter and putting it handy to the mixer?" he asked.

Lois did as requested. John continually increased the heat as the water boiled off, and the boiling volume of the mixture decreased. His main concern was to avoid a boil-over. Eventually he took the sugar/milk mix off the stove and asked Lois to dump the butter in while he kept stirring.

"You have to cook the sugar/milk mix long enough to boil off enough water to get the temperature up to about 235°/238°F. If you don't get rid of enough water, the fudge will be too soft to handle at room temperature, and it gets all over your fingers."

He continued stirring a few more seconds, then said, "If you dump the butter into the saucepan, the residual heat in the bottom of the pan goes into warming and melting the butter. If you have the butter waiting in the mixer bowl — cold — and try to pour the sugar/milk mix over it, the last of the sugar/milk mix to leave the pan will be burnt by the excess heat in the pan bottom. So we put the butter in the saucepan, to use some of the heat to good effect. Putting the butter into the mix at this stage also seems to make the whole mess come out of the saucepan easier."

John stirred the mass until the butter melted into the sugar and milk, then poured the lot into the mixer bowl, scraping the last of it out with a spatula. Turning on the mixer, he dumped in the chocolate chips. In three or four minutes, the mixer had blended the chocolate with the other ingredients into a thick homogeneous mass.

"Now, in go the marshmallows," he said. The mixer soon had the puffy little white balls completely integrated into the mixture. Two tablespoons of vanilla extract finished off the additions.
"… everything to excess…" John said with a grin, tipping in just a hair more, directly from the vanilla bottle. The mixer took another minute or so to blend everything together smoothly.

John then dumped in the nuts, and mixed them in by hand. He grinned at Lois as he did so.

"You don't need me to tell you that you don't want to use the mixer to blend stuff like nuts into a mess like this — the mixer would break them up too small."

Lois nodded, and smiled.

"I used to do ALL the mixing by hand when I was a kid," John said to Pete, who had strolled into the kitchen. "You'd think the marshmallows were never going to melt, but they always did in the end. Builds muscle, my dad used to say."

"Whatcha makin'?" Pete asked, before he could stop himself from responding.

"Chocolate fudge. The best you'll ever taste," John said. "If you read about making fudge in a cook book, you'd never try it, they make it sound so complicated. About the only way to spoil this stuff would be to burn the sugar/milk mix while you're cooking off the water, but if you stir it constantly, that won't happen."

"You said you'd made this fudge lots of times before…?" Lois asked. John was now pouring the fudge into the greased glass pan, using a spatula to keep the thick hot mass moving and spreading evenly.

"I used to make fudge when I was a kid in school. I started about Grade 7, I guess. Pretty soon I had several regular customers, including five bakeries and two restaurants. I always had a pack at school, and I had plenty of buyers among my friends at school. I made more money off my fudge than any kid I knew who had a paper route. I used to go through a 40 pound box of chocolate chips every couple of months!" While he was talking he carried the pan out to the screened-in porch where it would cool quickly in the chilly air.

"By morning it'd be cold right here in the kitchen, but this way we'll get to have some tonight. In an hour, maybe." He handed Lois the spatula to lick and offered Pete the mixer paddle for the same purpose.

Pete resumed his hostile attitude. "That's dumb! Why make it when ya can buy it?!"

"Well, go ahead." John said, licking the mixer paddle himself. "Walk into Kamloops and buy some if you want to. You don't need to eat any of this stuff."

Pete slouched off to the living room, out of hearing.

"He didn't mean it, John," Lois interceded. "All he did was ask a question."

"Yes he did. I just didn't like the tone of voice he used. He thought he could get me to argue with him. No dice! When he uses that tone of voice with me, it'll get him nowhere. The sooner he learns that, the easier it'll be for him."

"But, he's not used to…" Lois' words trailed off.

"Discipline and courtesy?" It was a blunt statement. "Then he's going to get acquainted with some of both while he's here. The Service Manager at the Jeep agency said it would be at least a week to fix your Jeep. You're welcome to stay here. Some company would do me good, too; I think sometimes I get a little ingrown, being here by myself. But I have rules, and one is civility. If he speaks to me civilly, I'll answer him the same way. Simple as that."

John began cleaning up the bowls and pans. Lois got the dish towel and pitched in.

"You might as well get used to it. Outside the big cities we don't take unwarranted guff from anybody. If Pete wants to know something, and asks me decently, I'll be happy to explain it to him."

Pete was sullen throughout the evening, while John and Lois had an animated conversation, ignoring him.

* * *

John picked up the letter and re-read parts of it. "…Peter is off with his friend, Larry, who is a decent boy. They went down to look at a boat a friend's father bought." And another sentence: "Peter is off the hook with the law — for now, at least. They gave him probation…" It must be tough, being a widowed mother with a boy in high school. There are plenty of good kids, but why does Peter gravitate to these no-goods?

His gaze moved back to the letter…. She thanked him for picking up the tab for getting the Jeep repaired. He had told her that he'd cover it, and she could reimburse him when she could. On the face of it that seemed pretty risky, but he had excused himself while the inspection was being made and the cost figured, and went up the street to his bank, to talk to Bill Mosier. He asked Bill to run a credit check on Lois Milner of Vancouver, giving him her address, place of employment, and her bank, which he'd extracted in conversation.

Of course, John couldn't get a credit check on anyone, but his banker could. Mosier got on the phone, and a few minutes later said, "She's not wealthy, but she pays her bills on time. Modest bank account, but has always been solvent. That tell you what you want to know? You loanin' her money?"

It was none of Bill's business, but John simply said, "I'm helpin' her out of a bind. Seems pretty solid, but thought I'd check first."

"Good idea. Friends can be the first to stiff you."

I didn't say she was a friend, John thought as he left the bank.

Lois was a computer medical transcriber at the University Hospital in Vancouver, and had a modest income, but she had said there was a little she could send each payday. The first couple of checks had arrived right on the dot.

The funny thing, John mused, was that Peter, during the six days it took to get the Jeep going again, had been quite tractable. He had been fascinated with John's collection of back issues of the homebuilt aircraft magazine Sport Aviation, and had begun asking John reasonable questions about them. Funny, but the kid seems to have some brains after all. Maybe what it takes….

Lois had apologized that the first check was so small, but her delay getting back to work had shortened her paycheck. She would send more in future installments. The enclosed check had been for a hundred dollars. From their conversations during her stay he gathered that she was just making it on her pay, and that one hundred dollars must have put quite a dent in it.

There had been plenty of time to talk during their stay. There were the normal chores to be done, as on any ranch, but she carried her end by fixing meals and keeping the house tidied up. There was plenty of room to accommodate them; his uncle's parents had raised a large family here, and John had given Lois and Peter two rooms out of the several he had closed off to save heat and firewood.

Conversation inevitably turned to their present lives and marital status.

"My husband, Allan, was an accountant with a law firm," Lois said. "He was hit in a crosswalk on his way to work. He died two days later." She sipped her coffee and reflected a few minutes.

"When we bought the house we had to borrow heavily against his insurance, and what we had left was eaten up by the funeral costs." She paused again, as though this was painful. "I was just getting back on my feet when Peter started running around with these dopers. I don't think he's into dope yet, but I'm afraid he will be if I can't get him away from them soon." She sat gazing out at the snow in silence.

It was John's turn to delve into his unpleasant marital past.

"I was married for just a little over a year, before my wife took 'French-leave.' She wasn't all that satisfied with the mundane life — and limited income — of a junior engineer with a small manufacturing firm. She liked parties, and I couldn't keep up with them. She disappeared one day, leaving a note that she'd be gone — permanently. She had found a more interesting life. That turned out to mean a wealthy playboy with a yacht and membership in the golf club. She'd met him while I was working one day. Dorie was never seen again — by me, at least. I received the divorce papers in the mail!" He did not add that he'd been happy to sign them, or that afterward he'd been pretty gun-shy with women.

He didn't feel entirely broken-hearted; she hadn't been all he'd expected; they had met in a romantic setting — rarely enough to make a marriage work. They really didn't know each other. Their values, it turned out, were at opposite ends of the spectrum. But it had been the way she left him that had got to him most.

* * *

Lois had been gone two and a half months, and strangely, John kept thinking of her. The memory of his previous venture into matrimony was a strong deterrent to future entanglements, though. Anyway, he had the ranch to run, and that was enough worry for now. Pete? He'd begun to like the kid, once he got rid of the smart-mouth attitude.

The other letter was from Richard Bowes, his hired hand. He usually only worked during the Spring, Summer and Fall, leaving to work in Kamloops during the Winter months. He had worked for Uncle Gilbert for many years, and John was glad to keep him on. But… the letter contained bad news: Richard had been working on his car — up on a jack — and with no blocks for safety. The predictable had happened, and Richard wouldn't be able to do any heavy work for some time — if ever. Geez! What am I going to do come Spring? The phone lines had been down for a few days this past week, hence the letter instead of a phone call.

John pondered how he was going to get the place back in shape without Richard. It was hard to find anyone to work this far out from "civilization." Richard had lived at the ranch during the week, and spent the weekends in Kamloops with his family. His kids were grown and gone, but the old man needed the work. He was a good worker, but in the couple of years that Uncle Gilbert had been sick, the ranch had gone downhill badly. Richard could do a good job, as long as someone was there to tell him what needed doing. What am I going to do without Richard? I can't do it all by myself!

The snow was still pretty deep and there wasn't much he could do in the way of making progress until it cleared, which was a month or two away. John fixed his supper and turned in after reading the latest Sport Aviation magazine, the publication of the Experimental Aircraft Association, a world-wide organization of people, both men and women, who build and fly their own airplanes.

He had become intrigued with flying, had taken flying lessons and received his Private Pilot's License after Dorie had taken her leave. Seeing several "homebuilts" at the airport at Kamloops, he had joined the EAA and was daydreaming of someday building one for himself. The price of "store-boughts" was high — out of proportion. Cessna and Piper, the Ford and Chevy of light private airplanes, had quit manufacturing single-engine private planes due to the proliferation of product liability lawsuits, which held the manufacturer liable for death or injury, no matter how negligent, stupid or drunk the pilot or other plaintiff might have been.

Chapter 2
Things are Different Here.

The phone woke him. He looked at the clock: it was 5:06 in the morning. Who the devil's calling at this hour? Haven't even got my coffee yet! John reached for the phone and grumbled a "Hello."

"John — it's Lois Milner — I'm sorry to bother you so early, but I just have to talk to someone. I just got Peter out of jail — he was arrested for vandalism! He was out with the Shugard brothers — they got hold of some liquor and did some damage — stupid kid stuff. The Shugard boys ran off, but Pete got caught, and now we have to go to court. I'm at my wits' end as to how to get Peter away from those boys." This was said breathlessly, as though she had been running. John recognized it as the exasperation it was, and the need for some steadying talk. She was on the edge of panic. It had been almost a month since her last letter, with another check…

A thought began creeping into his mind.

"Lois, let me get some coffee and get my other eye open, and I'll call you back in a while — OK?"

She agreed, and a few minutes later John sat down with a coffee and began making a list of things that needed to be done to get the ranch back on a paying basis. He called the airport in Kamloops for weather info between there and Vancouver, and checked on the availability of a Cessna. There was a 150 he could rent for a couple of days. It would do fine for his trip.

"Lois? John here. I have a thought on what we might be able to do with Pete. I'm going to come down to Vancouver so we can talk. Can you pick me up at Langley Airport, say about five this afternoon?"

"But, what airline will you be coming in on?" She sounded puzzled, knowing that virtually all passenger traffic in and out of Vancouver went through Vancouver International Airport.

"No airline. I'll be flying a rented airplane. Meet me in the General Aviation lounge. If I'm a little late, don't worry — the weather is reported to be good between here and there, but I may have to dodge a few bad spots. I'll see you about 5, OK?"

"Do you fly?" She sounded incredulous.

"Well, I have to have an airplane to do it, but yes, I fly."

He grinned at her surprise at civil air travel being for individuals as well as corporations. In this back country where roads were sometimes non-existent or treacherous, a private airplane was often the best way to keep track of land and livestock conditions. And for trips into town. John intended to have his own plane — someday.

Lois met him at the General Aviation Lounge at Langley Airport, and drove him to her home, a modest cottage in East Vancouver. Peter was with her late husband's parents for the afternoon, while she picked John up. This gave them some time alone to discuss Pete's problems on the drive back from Langley, and over a simple crockpot supper which she had put to cook before leaving the house.

"I feel guilty involving you in our troubles. After all, you didn't adopt us. But you seem to be the only one who has been able to penetrate Peter's armor at all. I'm at the end of my rope. Any more trouble and the court will start viewing him as an incorrigible, and there'll be no more lenient sentences. He's on probation, and his probation officer told me the only course that will work is to separate

Peter from the Shugards and their friends. I don't know how to do that. Without a strong man to keep him in line, he's surely going to be in jail within another few months. Do you have any thoughts on how I can handle it?"

"I may have something," he said. He told her of the letter from Richard, and its implications for getting the ranch back in shape.

"What I was thinking was to hire Peter to work at the ranch for his room and board, and some spending money. He can finish his school year at Barriere. They have a no-nonsense school there that I think is as good as any. He'll work around the ranch on weekends and after school, and do his homework in the evenings. The TV there isn't what he likes, anyway, so that interference won't be a problem. What do you think?"

*   *   *

The next day finished up late, after attending to arrangements which had taken most of the day, what with the probation officer and school. Records had been picked up at the school, and all the legal papers had been filled out and filed to give John legal authority to take care of injuries, medications and similar details inherent in taking over custody of a minor. Pete's luggage allowance for the trip was limited, as the Cessna was a rather small airplane. Lois was going to box up additional clothing etc. and ship them in a couple of days.

John laid it out in simple terms for Pete.

"Here's the deal, my friend. You've been playin' the fool here. The scrapes you've been getting into are a one-way ticket to prison. The Shugards have made a sucker out of you, and they'll let you take the rap for it. I've read what the judge wrote, and believe me, they're through playin' with you. We're not just talking juvenile stuff — the next time you come up in front of a judge, you'll be going to jail for some hard time! And it won't be a couple weeks in the city lockup. You'll do at least six months with the bad boys — the forty-year-old bad boys! What I offer is a chance to turn that around and clear your slate; get away from the guys you've been running with, and make something of yourself. Your mother has agreed with my plan.

"You'll live on the ranch with me, and help me get the place ready for Spring. You'll be going to school in Barriere, a small town a few miles east of my place. We have a bus, run by a rancher's wife, that comes by there and takes the kids into Barriere and brings them home every day after school. On weekends — and some afternoons and evenings — I'll need your help shaping the place up. I still have to figure out what I'm going to do with it. Cattle prices aren't too good right now, the herd's too small for any profit, and my uncle let it run down pretty badly. He was sick, so I can't blame him. But now it's mine, and I aim to get it into top shape.

"Your pay will be room and board, and a little spending money. Compared with life in the big city, you may think it's pretty boring, but it's better than prison any day. I'll be making weekly reports to your probation officer, and I'm going to be honest with him. I know you're puzzled about all this, but it boils down to a simple set of needs: I need help on the ranch. My hired hand was badly injured in an accident, and will probably never be able to work for me again. And you need to get away from the bunch you've been hanging out with before you get into real trouble. Do you understand me so far?"

A sullen nod was all the answer John got before Pete slouched off to his room.

* * *

The flight back to Kamloops was a little bumpy, but Pete's enthusiasm for his first taste of flying turned him into an avid student. After explaining the basics of flight and control, John turned the control wheel and pedals over to him. At first Pete over-controlled all over the sky, but within a few minutes he was able to hold it straight and level and hold a reasonable facsimile of a course. His original panic about flying in a small plane had disappeared.

John took the controls back as he called the Kamloops tower to report position and ask for approach clearance. By the time they had Pete's couple of bags in the pickup, Pete was babbling one question after another about flying. This might turn out better than I thought, John mused between answers. This kid's brighter than he seemed the last time he was here.

"If you've got a jacket of some kind, you can hang it on one of the nails here by the door," John said as they entered the ranch house kitchen.

The neck of Pete's duffel bag was closed with what at first glance appeared to be a few wraps of rope, but what was in fact a knot. Pete opened the bag, extracted a coat, and hung it on one of the nails John had indicated.

Twisting the neck of the duffel bag shut, he gave the knot a practiced jerk with both hands. The knot tightened up and stayed that way.

"Hey — that looks like a good trick! What've you got there?" John asked, openly impressed.

"It's a Jug Sling Knot. My Dad taught me how to tie it when I was just a little kid. He made this duffel bag when he was in the Navy. Most people would've put eyelets in the neck, and put a draw-string on it, but a jug sling knot works just as good — if you know how to tie one."

"Would you show me how to tie it?" John's interest was obvious. Nor had he failed to notice the note of pride in the boy's voice, and the slight change in manner that had just manifested itself.

"Sure." Pete loosened the knot, pulled it off the neck of the duffel bag, and untied it.

"There's two ways to tie it, and both of them are tricky — you gotta pay attention to your knittin', as my Dad used to say…"

Pete's demeanor changed from sullen kid to sure-of-himself equal as he showed John how to tie the knot. After seven or eight tries, John had it down pat.

"Now that is cool, Pete — I like that!"

Pete grinned, retied the knot, and slipped it back onto the neck of his duffle bag.

"Yeah — it IS." The last word came out with a bit of a grunt as he gave the knot that same quick pull to tighten it on the bag with finality. "It's also a good knot to use if you want to put a hang-up loop on a glass bottle — which is why they call it a Jug Sling Knot — and it'll never come loose unless you want it to."

Later, after supper at the ranch, as John headed to his own room he saw Pete unpacking his meager belongings.

"Looks like we're going to have to get you some clothes more suitable for living out here. We'll go into Kamloops tomorrow morning and then out to Barriere to get you set up in school."

A sullen grunt from Pete acknowledged this, and John went to his room feeling that he might have bitten off more than he wanted to chew.

However, as he drifted off to sleep, he smiled to himself, wondering how long it would be before Pete noticed the knot on the hackamores he and Uncle Gil had always used on the ranch's saddle horses. There, it's called a double hackamore knot, but it's the same knot.

*   *   *

John was grading out the drainage ditch along the road when the bus dropped Pete off beside the dozer.

"What're ya doin' that for?" was Pete's greeting. He was still sullen.

"My uncle Gil had a flood early one Spring when a warm spell combined with a warm rain melted the snow above the ranch. The runoff overflowed the ditch and cut a channel across the ranch, damaging that shed over there, and nearly getting into the basement where Aunt Louise stored the preserves, potatoes and other things. If the runoff had reached there it would have ruined a lot of food, as well as the house's central heating."

"So what!" Pete slouched off toward the house half a mile away.

John was dust from head to toe, and dog tired. The weather had turned warmer than the time of year warranted, and the potential for another flood worried him. Much of the snow on the flat had melted, but there was still plenty up on the mountain. He again glanced toward the ridge a mile behind the house.

"Up to your butt in mud and dust blowing in your eyes!" John muttered. Pete's sullen mood was getting to him! It had been this way the entire week since he'd brought the boy home with him.

Maybe I made a mistake, he mused as the Cat wrassled another blade-full of mud up onto the bank. This wasn't the best machine for the job, but it was what he had. That kid has to settle down sometime. How long does a sulk last?

John had showered and changed clothes, and came down to start fixing dinner. As he walked into the kitchen he found Pete rummaging through the kitchen cupboards.

"What're you looking for, Pete?" he inquired.

"Lookin' for something to drink," the boy retorted, in his usual tone.

"Well, there's milk in the fridge, and a case of Coke out on the screen porch. They're cold."

"I don' want any of that crap! I want somethin' worth swallowin'."

"Booze."

"Yeah, why not?"

"You're out of luck. I don't keep any around. Besides, what makes you think I'd let you have any?"

"You can't stop me! You ain't my dad! You're just some sucker do-gooder."

"I run this place, and I can stop you." John had started fixing the dinner. "Besides, there isn't any here, so I guess you're out of luck!"

"You sumbitch! I c'n lick you any time," and Pete suited action to words, hurling a punch at John from behind. John got a flicker of it reflected from the window, and the punch bounced off his shrugged shoulder. Dropping the knife into the sink, he whirled, lowering his left fist to near the floor and bringing it up with his legs behind it into the kid's belly. The punch sounded like a dropped sack of rice. Pete was propelled backwards, thoroughly doubled over. Gasping for air, he spewed vomit across the floor. Crumpling against the far wall, he sat gasping and throwing up.

John returned to the matter of peeling the spuds. "When you feel up to it, clean up every last bit of your puke, and then get yourself cleaned up for dinner."

A very subdued Pete did as he was told, and twenty minutes later quietly sat down at the table. There was no lively conversation during dinner this night. Of course, there hadn't been on any other night since Pete's arrival, so in that respect things were little different than before.

Dishes done, John got out the video tape his friend in Kamloops had lent him of the fly-in at Oshkosh, Wisconsin, the previous August. Every year the EAA holds their fly-in there, and "homebuilders" from around the world come to show off their own creations, admire others', and generally have fun. Wittman Field is, for that one week, the busiest airport in the world. And the most fun.

Being the headquarters of the EAA, there are hundreds of aircraft, from sophisticated multi-engine "store-boughts" to hyper-aerobatic air-show craft, replica World War One and Two fighters — plus some real ones. If it flies, you'll see it at Oshkosh.

The TV was emitting sweet sounds of big round engines and the howl of over-speeding propellers as the video focussed in on a three-plane flight of T-6s streaking across the screen. Out of the corner of his eye John saw Pete quietly slip into a chair in a far corner of the room.

After a few minutes John said, "You can see better from over here," pointing to a chair a few feet from his own.

Pete silently moved to it and they both sat entranced with the pictures.

* * *

Saturday was a long day. It was Pete's second Saturday, and he was finding out what real work was like; John had taken it easy on him his first Saturday and Sunday. He had received a phone call from Carl Buehler, a rancher up the valley, asking if John had enough grass to feed 150 steers until June. He had them sold, but the buyer didn't want them until then, and Buehler had a herd of ewes that had lambed in March, and his lot was already too full. He wanted to move the steers out and use it for the sheep. Given the current poor price of cattle, he had held onto the steers, hoping for the price to go up, but now he was in a bind for space.

John was more than willing to board Carl Buehler's steers. It wasn't much, but it would mean some cash income — of which he hadn't seen much lately. His own herd wasn't large, but he didn't want to mix them — he didn't want to have to cut them out come June. So, the line of post holes was creeping across the south third of the ranch.

John also had an ulterior motive; the price of sheep on the hoof was getting better, and should do well this year. His own ewes had also lambed, and his brother Garry had told him that the Wavell Packing

House in Washington had a very large order from an Arabian sheikh for two thousand mature sheep and one thousand lambs, on the hoof. The buyer, Wavell, would provide the trucking, so that worry wasn't his. They were going to ship this Fall from Seattle, and Garry had secured an option for all John could buy and produce. This would not bring in any large amount of cash until Fall, but the boarding of Buehler's stock would help tide him over until then. There would be increment payments as he acquired the stock, but the final payment wasn't until shipment.

Pete was back to his sullen mood, but dripping sweat as he wrestled posts onto the flatbed and drove it to the line of holes John was digging with a tractor-mounted auger. Dropping one post into each hole and pulling forward to the next, climbing down and wrestling a post into that hole, and then the next…. His heavy gloves were wringing wet from sweat.

After dropping the last post off, he drove to the pickup where the water jug sat on top of the saddle toolbox. Squatting a little, he reached up and pressed the button, and let the cold water stream into his mouth, swallowing gulp after gulp. He'd never been so thirsty. And no water had ever tasted quite so good. He let some of it run onto his head and tousled his hair to spread it around. It felt good!

Glancing up, he grinned as he saw John approaching on the Cat. Then he remembered to be sullen again. He clambered up into the flatbed's cab and started off for another load of posts.

The "bob-wire" was strung, lying on the ground, when they knocked off for the day. The shower sure felt good! Rubbing down afterward he chuckled. Bet the Shugard boys couldn't've done what I done today! Then he remembered that he was being exploited — at least that's what he thought was the right word.

Sunday morning John had him up early. "Why?" was his only, but surly, comment.

"It's Sunday. We're goin' to church."

26

"I don't go to church!"

"You do now, Pal", was the rejoinder. With much complaining he got into what passed for his "Sunday best," and the two drove into Barriere. John was greeted by everyone they met; in a small town everybody knows everyone else, and he introduced Pete as a friend who had come to stay at the ranch for a year or two — get to see what ranch life was like and all that.

Pete had been worried that he'd run into some of the boys from school, where he'd been trying to establish himself as a "man from the big city." He did, but none of them seemed to have been impressed. They welcomed him as they would a friend of an old friend. This didn't help his "I'm-being-picked-on" attitude. In fact he seemed to find that they and he did have things in common, talking about little things about life on a ranch.

After church, he and three of the other boys were talking, and Pete mentioned the Oshkosh video. At first the others were skeptical, but soon he had them convinced.

"Maybe we can watch it sometime," Larry said, hopefully. The other two chimed in, and Pete said he'd ask John. Maybe some evening....

Then there was Shirley. She was a tall auburn-haired girl with a mischievous smile for him, and he was smitten. He had met her at church, and wanted to see more of her, but she lived the other side of Barriere.

*   *   *

The "bob-wire" was stapled to the posts when the two sweaty workers drained the last of the water from the "jimmy-john," again dousing their hair. It had been a long afternoon.

"I don't like working on Sunday, but this time of year, and with no help during the week, it's got to be done," John said. "I can finish the gate tomorrow, and Buehler's hands will be driving the steers in about four tomorrow. Thanks for the help, Pete. I never would have got it done in time by myself."

Pete grinned, the grin of comradeship between two tired men after a day's work.

"John, a couple of the boys want to see the Oshkosh video. Think maybe they can come over some night and see it?" He didn't realize he had dropped the sullen slurring speech.

"Don't see why not. Get on the phone after dinner and set up a night. Their dads too, if they want."

The easy, relaxed attitude lasted the rest of the evening. Maybe this'll work after all, John mused as he drifted off to sleep.

*　*　*

Pete had never ridden a horse. He'd never even been near one. But if he was going to work on a cattle ranch, handling horses was something he was going to have to learn. Buehler's herd was keeping him busy afternoons, hauling hay out to the fenced-off spread, since there wasn't much grass up yet, and his muscles were developing. Lift this, carry that over there, take this out to the tractor and bring back the black toolbox.

John now had him feeding and rubbing down Red and two other horses every day. One was a quiet line-back buckskin gelding that Pete had taken a liking to; last Sunday afternoon John had taught him how to saddle and bridle him, and then he got his first taste of the saddle. At first he had been wary, but the animal had seemed willing enough, and John's coaching soon had him feeling at home on the buckskin. Of course, that had all been in the home lot, in a corral, and he had his first ride in open country to come.

After four weeks of ranch life with plenty of physical work after school, he was getting to feel less fatigued when he hit the sack, and his muscles ached less every morning. He also now knew how to run a temporary water line to the new water trough in the "Beuhler

Compound," as John had dubbed it. The day before, he had climbed the windmill tower to grease the gearbox.

Every day had him learning some new kind of work — and then getting to put in the rest of daylight doing it. At first he'd felt kind of dumb, with John having to teach him all these things, but now he felt a nudge of pride at all he had learned to do. He'd considered himself pretty smart in the city, but that was growing dim. The things he used to think were so important now seemed like so much kid stuff.

John stuck his head in Pete's door and announced, "I just got off the phone with Jerry Johnson at the airport. I have to go into Kamloops for supplies Saturday, and thought I'd better get in a couple hours in a Cessna. Have to stay current, you know. Want to go?"

That was a silly question. "Yeah!" Pete all but shouted. "Can I fly it some, too?"

"I just might let you. You've earned a bit of R and R."

Pete had never dreamed that someday he would actually handle the controls of a plane high above the ground — and now he'd already had a taste of it. Bet the Shugard boys would think it's dumb, but they don't know nuthin'! Hey! I used to think I wanted to impress them that I could do stuff — stupid stuff — as good as they could....

Saturday arrived and, with business done, John drove to the airport.

"Hi, Jerry, is the bird back in yet?" It had been rented for a while earlier that morning but was due back.

"Not yet. Any time now. Got time for a 'burger?" He nodded to Pete in greeting.

"Why not?" The three of them headed for the cafe. Every airport has to have a cafe, and here was no exception.

Pete smelled the gasoline and a sniff of lacquer — someone was painting an airplane. He savored the airport smells — paint, gasoline, tires, greasy engines, and clean ones smelling of "gunk," the solvent universally used. A fresh wind blew across the field and he stopped to watch a blue and yellow biplane just ready to touch its wheels to the pavement.

"What kind is that?" he asked John.

"Stearman. It was the U.S.'s basic training plane during the war. Great airplane; I've flown it once. Belongs to Alex Harper. We'll take a closer look at it when we get back."

* * *

"OK, you take it off. Wind's straight down the runway, so no correction's needed. Remember, just take everything easy. Ease the throttle open all the way, and keep your hand on it until you're well off the ground, and if you lose directional control, simply pull the throttle all the way back. I'll take care of the rest of it. Keep it headed straight down the runway with your rudder pedals. Easy does it." John checked the pattern for any inbound aircraft. "Okay, let 'er roll!

"It'll feel like it wants to fly, but keep it on the ground by very slight forward pressure on the wheel until it tells you it really wants to fly, then let it. Ease back slightly on the wheel and keep her headed straight as we climb…. Hold the airspeed at 70. That's it. Trim the nose up a mite to keep her at 70. Great!" The Cessna held a steady climb to about 800 feet above the ground.

"Now, gently turn the wheel left — just until she banks — just about so," making a plane of his hand. "Now, ease a little left rudder to start her turning, then neutral, and maybe a little right to keep her nose up. See, you've increased her bank, so you'll want a little more right rudder to keep her nose up. That's it. Easy… Great…"

Half an hour later they were over the ranch. Pete was still flying the Cessna, and John was pointing out the lay of the land to him and occasionally clicking his camera. The ridge behind the house passed beneath their wings and John pointed to the radio towers on the highest peak. "That's where the road leads to that you and your mom got stuck on. About all there is up there is those radio and telephone repeaters — and some good hunting country. Ever been hunting?"

"No. I've never even shot a gun."

"I'll teach you — the right way." John left it at that.

Two hours were gone like seconds to both of them. For those who love to fly, that's the way it is. John got clearance to land from the tower, greased the gear on, and taxied to Jerry's ramp. The fuel truck came over and John showed Pete the business of fueling the bird. Last night, John had gone over the basics of flight; the weight-versus-lift and thrust-versus-drag things. He had shown him the pre-flight inspection before they took off and described the functions of the controls. Today was really overloading Pete's memory banks.

* * *

"We went flying today, Mom, and I got to fly it most of the time. It was great…" The adjectives tumbled out as he made his regular week-end phone call to his mother. "John let me take it off and then we flew over the ranch and saw the road where we got stuck that day, and…".

John was out in the barn, and didn't get to talk with Lois, but he generally got in a few words, most Saturday night calls. Newsy, but he kept things at a low key. Pete was doing very well, compared with his first week or two, but he had his moments.

There were times he sat alone moodily, and seemed to be missing his friends back in the city. What John didn't realize, and couldn't know, was that Pete was pondering his former lack of common sense, some of the stupid things he'd done, and wondering if he were quite up to par with the rest of civilization. It was more introspection than surliness now.

One day at school, Pete was feeling some of the old urge to impress someone with his street-smart ways. Bob Keenawah was a Nez Perce Indian — tall, a good athlete and got good grades. Another ranch kid, he was one of the group of boys of the same age group that spent their after-school time together while waiting for the bus. Bob asked Pete where he had previously lived, and Pete told him. Bob asked, "What do you do there for fun?"

Pete thought for a moment and said, "We hang out. Couple months ago me an' the Shugard boys borrowed a ride, drove around town. Benny was drivin' an' he took a corner kinda fast, an' creamed a parked car. We got a busted wheel an' took off. They never caught us."

Bob wrinkled his nose. He said in an offended voice, "You stole a car?"

"We just grabbed it for a ride! We was gonna take it back."

"I don't care if you rode it in the rodeo, that's theft! Are you a thief?"

"Hell no, I'm not a thief! I told you we just borrowed it."

"I don't care what you said it was — it's theft!" Bob turned to the other boys, "Watch your backs, we got a thief in our midst!"

Pete grabbed Bob's arm and swung him around. "Don't you call me a thief!" and took a roundhouse swing at him. The punch landed but didn't seem to faze Bob in the least.

He reached out and grabbed a handful of shirt-front and yanked Pete up to him so hard their faces nearly touched. "You do something like that again Mister, I'll clean the road with ya!"

Pete struggled to regain his footing when Bob let go; he wasn't that much smaller than Bob, but Bob suddenly seemed much bigger.

"Let me tell you something, kid. Things are different up here. An' we like it that way. You play any of those games around here an' you can forget about havin' any friends. Get me?"

The bus ride home was pure misery; none of the rest of the kids even looked at Pete, let alone spoke to him.

Chapter 3
There's No Such Thing as an Empty Gun

At dinner Pete was withdrawn. After dinner John said, "Lets go into the living room. I think you have something you need to talk about."

John sat in his uncle's old LazyBoy, and Pete sat on the couch opposite. He sat quietly for several minutes and John let him have his time.

Finally Pete said, "How'd you know?"

"Just from the way you're acting. You don't have to tell me if you don't want to."

"I want to," Pete said, hesitating and then going ahead. "I did something really dumb after school today. We were all talking and Bob asked me what we did for fun in Vancouver."

He went on to tell John the details, not sparing himself a bit. When he was finished they sat in silence for another few minutes.

"What can I do now? I guess I sort of screwed myself up with the guys, didn't I?"

"Well, it took some guts to lay it out to me like you just did. Things are different out here. That's the main reason I thought of having you come and stay with me. There's a lot of temptation in a city to be like everyone else — at least those you hang out with. Out here, there's room to think and lots of space, and a thief can probably get away with a lot before he's caught. But the values are different here. Friendships are built on trust. We don't need a cop on every corner.

"People like you for what you are — or aren't. Maybe to steal something — no matter what you call it — in the city and among that type of gang, is considered 'cool.' Not out here! People still respect honesty and courage here.

"Now, here's what you do. Go up to Bob tomorrow morning and just flat apologize. No ifs, ands or buts. In front of others. Tell him you were wrong. Tell him that you came to live with me because your friends in the city were getting into that kind of thing, and you weren't happy with it. You told them about the car thing because he asked what you did for fun in the city, and you used to think it was smart. You don't now. Then ask to shake hands and forget it. See what he does."

"You think he'll accept it?" Pete was dubious.

"You're not dealing with the Shugard boys. I know Bob and his dad. They're good people. Get to know Bob and you'll like him. Do you know the story of Chief Joseph?"

"Is that in the Bible?"

John laughed, "Not hardly! A different Joseph. Chief Joseph was the leader of the Nez Perce Indians, and after a long and arduous war with the American Army, he retreated into Canada, giving a promise that, 'I will fight no more from where the sun now stands, forever.' The Nez Perce's settled all throughout this part of Canada. Bob and his family are descendants of Chief Joseph's tribe. They live about ten miles further up the road."

Pete spent the rest of the evening doing homework, while John wrote some letters.

*　*　*

36

John set several tin cans along a 2x4 laid across two rocks about 50 yards in front of the shooting bench. Back at the bench he showed Pete how to load the 22 rifle. It was a Winchester Model 69A, with a five-shot magazine, but John was loading it as a single shot for this training session. He sighted the little rifle on the end can and squeezed the trigger. The loud crack made Pete jump, and the can spun off the board. John worked the bolt, loaded it again, sighted, fired, and the second can spun away.

He handed the rifle to Pete, the muzzle always pointed down-range. Pete had been shown how to insert the cartridge and close the bolt, and he did that, raising the rifle and sighting it as John had gone over with him the night before. The loud crack caused him to jump, and the can was safe — for the moment. The next round took a splinter out of the 2x4 an inch left of the target can.

John took the rifle from Pete. "Now I'll load it, and then you shoot it. Don't watch me load it." John said, turning away so Pete couldn't see what he was doing. Handing the rifle back to the boy, he said, "Now let 'er have it!"

Pete squeezed the trigger, but there was no loud crack, just a click. But the muzzle jumped a couple of inches!

"See — you're flinching," John said. "Give me the rifle again. In shooting circles we call this our kind of Russian Roulette. It's a good training method, and has nothing to do with suicide."

He took the rifle, put the empty cartridge back into the chamber, put it to his shoulder and squeezed the trigger. There was no "muzzle-jump."

"See, if you're anticipating the sound and recoil, you'll flinch. Squeeze the trigger smoothly so that when it goes off it surprises you. Concentrate on the target and your sights; there's no recoil to speak of with a .22. Now try it. And always put an empty into the chamber of a .22, or any rimfire, before you snap it, to protect the firing pin. You'll bust 'em, otherwise."

Pete loaded and fired, and the can spun off the board. Pete laid the rifle on the bench and started forward to inspect the can. John called him back sharply.

"Whenever you put a gun down, you first open the action and make sure it's empty. That's a habit you get and keep; it's not optional! A firearm is not a toy; you have to respect it and treat it with care. There is no such thing as an empty gun! Go back and open the bolt!"

Pete complied and John said, "Now it's OK to go forward." His grin took the sting out of his words.

*   *   *

It was a week later, and this time John had a Winchester .30-30. Again, the evening before, he had sat Pete down and gone over the operation and safety procedures of the lever gun. He had taken Pete to his loading bench in the basement, shown him how cartridges were loaded, and familiarized him with disassembly and assembly of the rifle. This was a "deer rifle" to most people, more complex and far more powerful than last week's .22.

Pete wasn't prepared for the recoil. The movies don't prepare a person for the real thing, and the blast and recoil rattled Pete's head. He hadn't remembered to hold the stock tightly against his shoulder, and he was going to be mildly black and blue there for a few days. He was game, though, and levered the second round into the chamber, sighted in, and this time the can flew into the air.

"Time to move the targets out further," John remarked.

Pete opened the action and laid the rifle on the bench before they went forward. Pete had good hand-eye coordination; he learned quickly, and John was a good instructor. By the end of the two-hour session Pete was logging one can per shot at a hundred yards.

The fired cartridges went into the cleaner that evening, and the next evening Pete learned how to reload the cartridges he'd fired.

"I'm getting a little tired of beef and pork. Ever have any rabbit?"

Pete shook his head. They were tucking away plates of beef stew, and, although it was good, a little variety would be welcome.

"Tomorrow's Sunday, so maybe after church we'll try to bag a few. What say?"

"Sounds good to me," Pete said, trying to sound casual. "Do we use the thirty-thirty?"

"You hit a rabbit with that and you'll have rabbit stew without having to cut him up," John laughed. "No, the .22 is the rifle for small game. I have two of them. I have a Remington single-shot you'll like. About the same as the Winchester otherwise, though."

The hike through the upland brush above the road up the mountain saw lots of small-game trails, but it was a while before a cottontail was sighted.

"Now watch me — how I do it," John said, silently moving for a clear shot. With a slow but steady movement he raised the rifle and took careful aim. The range was about seventy yards. The loud crack was followed by the rabbit jumping high into the air and falling into a clump of brush.

The two went forward and retrieved the game, and now it was up to Pete to bag the next one. He was nervous, but determined not to forget anything John had taught him about shooting. Ten minutes later John pointed out a cottontail just in front of a clump of rocks. Pete zeroed in and squeezed the trigger and the rabbit simply keeled over, a clean head-shot.

"That ought to be enough for tonight's dinner. It'll be getting dark by the time we get home. Besides, never shoot anything you don't plan to eat. There's plenty of them out here, and we don't need to put any in the locker. They taste better fresh, I think."

When they got to John's Land Cruiser, John made sure Pete unloaded his rifle before they put them in the vehicle. That evening Pete learned how to clean and skin the rabbits, and to top the day off John taught him how to fry them. He didn't need any lessons on eating the tasty meat.

*   *   *

The next Saturday John said they could stand having some more meat in the locker, and explained that, for rural residents, hunting deer or elk on your own property was legal most of the year.

John went to the rifle rack under the stairs and brought out two rifles. One was the .30-30 Model 94 lever gun Pete had been practicing with, and reloading for, for some time now.

The other rifle was a pre-64 Winchester 70. "My friend," he said to Pete, rubbing the stock affectionately.

"How long have you had that?" Pete asked, sensing there was a story here.

John opened the bolt, and handed the Model 70 to Pete.

"I bought this rifle when I was 17. Somebody had tried to glass bed it, but tightened the bedding screws unevenly before he set it aside for the epoxy to cure. The job was a botch, and naturally it tossed bullets all over the map afterwards. Dad took it in on a trade — he had a pretty good idea what was the matter with it. I bought it, re-stocked it under my dad's coaching, and we worked it over until it shot properly. Old Colonel Townsend Whelen called the Model 70 "The Rifleman's Rifle," and let me tell ya, Pete, I would bet my life on this one any day, anywhere, against any animal that walks this continent."

"What caliber is it?" Pete asked.

"30-06. It's a much more powerful round than the 30-30 there, but the little old 30/30 is the better choice for someone of your size and weight."

"Who's Colonel Townsend...?"

"Townsend Whelen. Col. Whelen was an old US Army boy that wrote a lot of good shooting stuff — magazine articles, and several books. I learned a lot from his writings. I've got some of his books around here — you can read 'em, if you like."

"Cool." said Pete approvingly, passing the Model 70 back to its owner.

John went into the living room and brought out the Fujinon binoculars to take with them. "Man! What a pair of glasses!" Pete exclaimed.

"They're something else, all right. Have a look."

Pete took the binoculars and put them to his eyes.

John recognized he'd never used binoculars before, when he clumsily tried to focus them. He showed Pete how to focus the individual eyepieces, while covering the front end of the other half of the instrument with the palm of the other hand, and leaving both eyes open.

"Holy smoke, I can see forever!" Pete pointed them at the radio tower on the ridge, fumbled with the focus, then, "Geez. I c'n see every piece of iron that tower's made of! Where'd ya get something like this?"

"They were given to me by a friend. They're really good ones; professional quality. I did him a favor once, a few years ago, and he gave me these in appreciation. They sure come in handy huntin'. Speaking of which, we'd better be gettin' out there if we're going to get any hunting in today."

Red and Mouse, the latter the name John had given to Pete's favorite, picked their way up the rutted road where Lois and Pete had made their debut, and then took a branch trail more steeply up the rocky hillside. Topping the ridge, they picked their way through the trees and scrub until they reached a saddle where they could see well into the valleys on each side of the ridge. Sitting their mounts, they searched both valleys and the slopes for deer or elk. The terrain was fairly heavily wooded and there was plenty of cover for four-legged critters.

"There's something moving over there," Pete sotto-voiced to John, pointing about 500 yards along and down the slope. John raised his glasses, and a minute later had a fix on a 5-point whitetail buck.

"I'll lead until we get into a better position and in range. Always be sure you see your game well enough to be sure it's what you really want to shoot — not some other hunter with camouflage. That deer is back in the brush enough that we can't tell whether he's standing side-on to us, or just has his head turned. If so, and you aim where you think the heart or lungs ought to be, you take a chance of just wounding him, and, although he might die later, you won't have meat for the locker. Plus it's a heck of a way for the animal to die — or live, wounded, crippled up and starving to death."

John leisurely led off on a circuitous route to keep trees between themselves and the deer, and thus not to startle it. Many minutes later John dismounted and ducked under some tree branches, crawling the last several yards to a spot behind a handful of head-size rocks. When Pete crawled up beside him, he saw they had a clean, side-on shot at their quarry, slightly less than a hundred yards away.

John whispered, "Slow! Raise your rifle and line your sights up on him. Pull the hammer to full-cock, and, when you're ready, fire." Pete did as he was directed. He was excited, and it took him four tries before he steadied the rifle enough, and squeezed the trigger.

The buck jumped forward a couple of yards, turned to look at them, and then turned to run away. As he turned, John's rifle spoke and the buck crumpled.

On inspection, they found Pete's bullet had hit too far back for a heart or lung wound. He'd probably have died shortly after, but by then the hunters might have lost track of him. John's bullet had angled into the chest cavity and finished the job.

John took the coiled rope he had tucked into his belt. Handing it to Pete, he said, "Chuck this over that limb on this tree — no — the one on the other side of the trunk. Yeah, that one," as the rope sailed over the branch.

"Now bring me the long end."

He took the rope and tied it around the roots of the deer's antlers.

"Now, you get over on the other end of the line and pull, while I drag from here."

Soon the buck was hanging from a stout tree branch, and John began showing Pete how to clean out a deer.

"You want to do it as soon as possible, otherwise the meat will develop a gamey taste."

After some more work with his knife he said, "When we skin him, we'll wrap the meat in the hide to take home. The parts that aren't good for eating we'll leave for the scavengers. They need to have a good feed once in awhile, too."

"What are the scavengers?"

"Coyotes, buzzards, crows, wolves — those sort of critters. Think what this world would be like if everything that dies just lay there and rotted. It takes all kinds of critters to keep a balance in this world."

"What about the head?" Pete asked.

"We'll leave it here for those same scavengers to pick clean, and next Fall we'll take it in and have the rack mounted."

Pete had a lot of things to ponder over, on the way home and in bed that night. His stomach was full of fresh liver, there was fresh venison in the locker, and he'd helped put it there. Wonder what the Shugard boys would think if they had seen me today! Sleep caught up with him before he had time to think that over.

* * *

Pete and Bob had become fast friends at school. Pete's straight-forward apology had earned him the respect of Bob and the rest of the class. It even cleared him of the thoughts that came and went about what if they found out about his being in trouble in Vancouver. Now it was out in the open, and nobody seemed to care — since he was honest about it.

One day Bob got off the bus at Pete's home — he'd come to consider it as that now. Pete had wanted to show Bob some of the Sport Aviation magazines, and Bob was interested. Bob had phoned home and his dad had said it was OK, he would come and pick Bob up when he was ready. He had borrowed a long-bladed chainsaw a while back, and wanted to return it to John, anyway.

"Look at this plane. Sort of scrawny-looking, isn't it?" It was an ultra-light made up of tubing, and translucent fabric covered wings and tail.

Bob said, "A fellow over the other side of Barriere has one something like that. He flies it quite a bit. One time he came clear over this way with it."

Pete turned the page to a photo of a Pitts S2A in flight, a picture obviously taken from a lead plane in close formation flight. "How'd you like to get into that and fly it!" He found himself talking as though he was an old timer at it. Well, at least I've flown a plane! Most kids my age haven't even been up in a small plane. And, John's taught me a lot about flying. His thoughts ran on while they thumbed pages.

"What's it like to be flying an airplane?" Bob asked.

"Oh, it's like nothing I've ever done before. When you get the bird lined up on the runway you push the throttle open and let her pick up speed. When you're going fast enough for the wings to create lift, the plane will let you know — it just feels like it wants to fly. So you ease the wheel back a little and…"

John was in the kitchen getting dinner started, and was hearing most of this, grinning from ear to ear. The old hand at flying! The boys' discourse continued until Bob's dad showed up with the chainsaw, and the two men went out to the barn to look at the post hole auger on the Cat that Evan wanted to see.

John told Evan about what he'd overheard. "Pete's been like that about flying ever since I brought him up here. Does pretty good at the controls, too. I guess he's a 'natural.' Some people are — they just take to it. He learned shooting right off the bat, too. Pretty sharp kid."

"Bob told me he had some trouble when he lived in Vancouver," Evan said. "Kin of yours?"

"No. He and his mother got stuck on that trace back there — the one going up to the repeater station — in a snowstorm. She got lost. Stayed a few days 'til she got her jeep fixed, and the kid and I took a liking to each other. He was running with the wrong bunch in Vancouver, and once that starts it's hard to break — hard for the kid, too. So, when my hired hand got hurt and couldn't work for me any more, I thought of hiring Pete to work for me. Works out good both ways. I can't afford a full-time hired hand, and Pete could stand a change of scenery."

Evan grinned, "Looks like you could stand havin' a woman, too. You're gettin' too old to be livin by yourself 'way out here. Makes a man kinda funny in the head after a while." He had been hinting for some time that John needed to get married. Mainly just teasing, but some sincerity in it, too. He was a thoroughly married type, with three boys and a girl, and just couldn't understand that a man could be happy any other way.

Evan was almost old enough to be John's father, and looked on John almost as another son. In fact, John had gone to a couple dances and a movie in Barriere with Nada, Bob's older sister, a long time ago. A very nice girl, but just didn't do anything for John in the romantic department. That was before Dorie, but he and Nada, although good friends, just felt nothing more personal about their relationship.

John grinned back and said, "You don't have any family members in mind, do you?" He knew that Nada had married Will Parker over the other side of Kamloops. "Nada's still married to Will, isn't she?"

"Yeah. Very much so! They have a two year old boy and another due in a month or two."

"Jeez! I didn't know I was hangin' around with a grandpa!" John chided. "Didn't realize you were that old."

"Just started early, I guess." The conversation drifted on to the D-8 Cat and the power-take-off mounted auger John and Pete had installed on it before they dug the postholes.

*　*　*

The weather had set in again. They would have a few more storms yet before Spring took a good hold, and this was one of them. Dinner was late, as they had been out clearing a drain from one of the fields to the "tank" — Texas type. John had dug a large dam and depression in the course of a swale to catch and hold the water for the cattle instead of letting it go on down toward the river. The last storm had clogged a part of the swale with brush and debris so that run-off was cutting a channel around where he wanted it to go. That done, they were ready for this storm, and it promised to be a lulu.

46

They were finishing dinner, and Pete cocked his head. "Listen. There's a plane up there in that soup."

The drone of a turboprop faded in and out in the dense, moist air above.

"He's really low, too," John added.

The drone passed westward and then ceased. There was an uncertain, muffled sound, and then nothing but the howl of the rising wind.

John went to the phone and dialed the Kamloops tower. "Has there been a plane flying around out about 40 miles north of you?"

"Yes. Do you hear him?"

"Not now. Just a minute or two ago we heard one, and then it went quiet. Has there been one in this area?"

"Yes. Right! Where are you?"

"This is Morgan Ranch, about four miles west of Highway 5, and about 2-1/2 miles south of Bonaparte Lake. Why?"

"We just lost a WesCan Airlines turboprop from our radar in that area."

"It was a turbo. I'm a pilot, and recognized it."

"We're afraid it's down. Do you have anyone there who can start a search?"

"Just me and my son," John didn't feel a need to get into an explanation of relationships. "I'll call a few of my neighbors, and then we'll start on up. I have a hand-held CB radio. I'll use channel 9. There's a ridge runs about a mile north and west from the ranch house. A bad road runs up to a pair of repeater stations directly west of the house on the ridge. Think you can find it from that?"

"Can do. Try to get word to us if you find anything at all, and we'll get a SAR op[1] in the works. Good luck. By the way, what's your name?"

"John Morgan. I own the Morgan ranch. Use it as your staging base. I'll leave the house unlocked so your people can get in. We'll get our gear together and get up there as soon as we can. We'll have to take horses — the road's too bad for my vehicles, and it peters out at the ridge."

He hung up the phone and turned to see Pete's eyes as large as saucers.

"Are we really going to go up there in this storm? Won't we get lost?"

---

1   Search and Rescue operation.

Chapter 4
In Daylight and by Moonlight

"I know that mountain like the back of my hand, day or night. And you've been hunting three times all over where we're going. Think of those people in that plane. If it went in, they're going to need help, and badly! Get into your long-johns — wear two pair — and get your heavy coat, then go out and saddle Red and that buckskin of yours."

Pete stood there in a sort of daze. John raised his voice to a bellow, "Get your ass in gear! There's people hurt! We're gonna try to help them — now MOVE!" Usually John avoided use of strong language, but he had to jolt Pete out of his shock.

John proceeded to follow the same instructions about dressing which he had given Pete. Pete had been galvanized into action with John's shouted command, and he was soon headed to the barn to saddle the horses. John continued to gather things he figured they'd need. He rolled four blankets and tied them with heavy cord. His first aid kit was a large industrial type, and he rigged it with rope to lash on one of the horses. He got out a small tarpaulin and from a cupboard got out two plastic bags and stuffed them full of coats and jackets. There would probably be many victims in shock, and they would need what warmth he could provide.

Lugging all this to the barn, he began lashing everything to Red and Mouse. From a cupboard in the barn he got three large battery lanterns and two long flashlights. Lashing the lanterns to the horses, he handed one flashlight to Pete, slipping the other into Red's saddlebag. Going back into the house, he broke open a cardboard box of chocolate bars and carried them out to the barn.

"Here, Pete. Split these up between our saddlebags. We'll probably be out a long time and we'll need the extra sugar to keep up our energy. Grab those canteens and fill them. Sling two on each horse. You 'bout ready?"

Pete nodded, and as soon as he returned with the canteens they mounted and rode out. The night was black as pitch, and a steady cold rain was slanting down from the west. They both wore the typical Western hats, which kept the rain from their heads, and their slickers kept them partially dry. A fine spatter of rain crept inside, though, enough to have them quickly shivering. How John was finding the way was black magic to Pete.

The ground began to slope upward a little, and increased as they rode. Pete thought to himself that a flash of lightning would be welcome to help see where they were, but the storm wasn't very cooperative. Pete lost track of time as the horses slogged steadily ahead, and he found himself dozing, miserable in the chill dampness that filled every crack and crevice in his clothing. Inside his gloves, his hands were numb from cold, and his breath hurt his lungs.

John looked at his watch with his flashlight. 10:35. They'd been on the trail over an hour — two hours since leaving the barn. At least another hour to the top — that's where John guessed the plane had gone in. A likely place, since the ridge was at its highest at the repeater towers, and it was likely that the plane was not quite high enough to clear the ridge. It had sounded to be in that direction, anyway.

Pete urged his horse up alongside John. "Let's go back. We'll never find them in this." He waved to describe the storm and trees.

"No way! There's people hurt, maybe dying. They need our help — yours and mine. We can't do much, but we'll do what we can. I'll try to radio back the location so others with rescue gear can find it quicker. There's no knowing how many lives depend on our doing the best we can."

Pete dropped back, his thinking swinging between pride that they were doing something important, and his wish to be home and dry and in bed. Oh, what a delightful spot bed would be right now!

What he could not know was what John was thinking. John was grinning inwardly to himself over recollections of another teenager riding this same mountain — this very slope — in daylight and by moonlight, and once even in a snowstorm, nearly thirty years before. His aunt had worried at his liking for night rides, but he had never come to grief, although there had been close calls — a dry jackpine branch had nearly whipped his eye out one night. Another evening he and his lineback buckskin gelding had had a minor encounter with a mother bear and her cub, which ended with both parties succeeding in going their own way without conflict. Mouse — Pete's horse — was not the loaded stick of dynamite Sancho had been, but lineback buckskins were often regarded as horses likely to be tough, and Mouse — a lineback like Sancho — was a fine horse, although much quieter than the one that ranged through John's memories this stormy night.

Those long-ago night rides had given John a confidence in himself that had steadied him through his high school years, and had etched into his mind a knowledge of this mountain that was for him now like a well-lit map on a clean table. What puzzled Pete was not black magic — John knew the mountain like the face of an old friend.

Another hour and they were nearing the towers. They passed the sign that pompously notified them they were trespassing on government property, and the dire results if they were caught. Peering carefully through the drizzle John spotted a slight lightening of the gloom off to the south. It flickered, rose and died. Fire!

"C'mon, Pete — there's a fire over there!" he shouted over his shoulder as he rode off along the game trail on the ridge toward the glow. It grew until, after about half a mile, they came on the scene of the disaster. The plane had impacted just below the ridge, and apparently had remained nearly intact, plowing through several treetops and heavy brush before contacting the rocky soil of the ridge. There were several rag-dolls lying around the plane, and a few of them were wandering dazedly about, peering at those on the ground in the nearly total darkness. John broke out his flashlight, turned it on and began waving it to attract the attention of those moving around.

As they entered the zone of wreckage and bodies, John tethered the horses to a tree and went ahead on foot. He approached the small group of shivering, miserable looking people and asked, "Is there a member of the crew that's up and around?"

"Yes. I'm Senior Cabin Attendant," a young woman answered. She limped forward, cradling an obviously broken arm. "Celia Young, sir."

"How many 'walking wounded' do you have?"

"Seventeen, in various modes of injury. Do you have a first aid kit with you, sir?"

"Yes." Turning to Pete who stood wide-eyed, "Get the first aid kit and bring it here, Pete." Pete strode off purposefully. Turning back to the attendant he asked, "How many aboard, including yourself and the rest of the crew?"

"Sixty four, sir. Can you help us?"

John hauled his CB radio from his coat and turned it on. Switching to channel 9, the emergency channel, he tried calling. "Breaker,

Channel niner. This is Morgan with a mayday. Does anybody copy?" He repeated it three times and then listened intently. He tried again, and listened. Nothing. Pressing the button again, he said, "Mayday, mayday, mayday. This is Morgan on Longbeard Ridge with a mayday. Over."

"Morgan, this is Kamloops tower. We read you two by 5. Say again your ten-twenty."

"Kamloops Tower, Morgan, half a mile — I repeat, one half mile southwest of repeater towers. Am at crash site. Total persons aboard, sixty four — I repeat numbers — six four. Walking wounded seventeen — I repeat numbers — one seven. Will begin checking for survivors and render what first aid possible. Rescue will need all-wheel drive vehicles to make it up the road. Road begins next to the farmhouse. Out."

"That's a roger, Morgan. Army Rescue party on way with military equipment. Will contact and advise them. Out, and thank you."

The chore of looking for bodies began. The fire was confined to the left wing, where a fuel tank still had some Jet A to burn. John guessed the other tanks had broken open and left their fuel behind in the trees.

Addressing the Cabin Attendant, he said, "Get what walking wounded that can help, and get some sort of shelter rigged under those trees. There's a tarp and blankets on the horses; have someone go get them and get the shelter started. I'm going to do a look-see through the fuselage for any still alive, and give them what first-aid I can. I'll try and rig a splint for your arm as soon as I see what shape those in the cabin are in."

Entering the fuselage — it was badly wrinkled but intact — John found a body on the floor, his head grotesquely smashed by impact. Pete, behind him, spun and threw up out the door. John grabbed the body by the coat shoulders and dragged it out the door and under the stub of the left wing, still a good way from the fire, which didn't show any signs of growing.

Re-entering the cabin, he found another man, seated and looking simply asleep. John touched him on the shoulder and he slumped forward, his head at an unnatural angle. Broken neck, probably. Feeling for a pulse, he found none, but since the body wasn't blocking access to others he left it where it was. Across the aisle was a woman, middle aged and matronly, who blinked her eyes and turning her head, looked at John. "Who're you?" she queried. "Are we there?"

"No, ma'am. You've crashed and I'm one of the first of the rescuers on the site. Can you get up?"

"I don't know. My legs hurt and they won't move. Can you help me up?"

"Maybe you'd better sit right there until the Army medics arrive. They're on their way now. If your legs are broken and we move you it might cause more injury. Can you sit there for a little longer?"

"Yes. But I have to go to the bathroom."

"I think it will be better if you have that kind of an accident rather than move broken legs. That's the least of your worries, and I don't think anyone will notice." As he stood up he noticed that Pete was right behind him.

"Good, Pete. I need you to help me. First we have to see how many are dead, then how many are alive and can move to get out of here, and how many are alive and have injuries bad enough to prevent being moved. This lady has broken legs, so we'll leave her sit here rather than risk greater injury by moving her."

"Yeah, I heard you talking with her. What do I do?"

"Just stay with me, and if we can help someone out of here, you help them get out and to shelter under the trees. Then come right back. You feeling all right now?"

"Yeah. I've never seen anybody dead before. Or hurt real bad. But I'm alright now. Go ahead, I'm behind you."

"Good man."

John proceeded up the aisle. Two more dead, then one with a pulse, but unconscious. John pulled the handkerchief out of the man's coat pocket and stuffed one end into his collar so half was hanging out.

"That marks him so rescuers will know he's alive but can't answer up," he explained to Pete over his shoulder.

John proceeded to a woman, apparently about thirty, dressed in a neat business suit. She had a pulse, but was also unconscious. John could see no visible injuries, and said to Pete, "Tear up a rag or something and mark her. Tuck a strip of white or light colored cloth in her collar so anyone coming from back by the door can see it."

Moving ahead he heard a snore, then a blowsy lady in her forties shook her head and looked around.

"Where are we? Wha's everybody doing?" Her breath reached John and he nearly passed out. Phew! What a load she must have had aboard!

"Are you alright? Can you move?" At her uncertain nod, he said, "Try standing up."

She did, wobbly, but was on her feet.

"Now, can you move out into the aisle?"

She did so, but stopped to let her head steady down.

"Pete, help the lady out and to the shelter." Pete took over and almost passed out from the fumes. But he disappeared through the door with her in tow.

The rest of the cabin went about the same, with dead mixed in with those alive but unable to help themselves. In the cockpit John found both pilot and first officer dead; they had been where the airplane took the worst beating coming through the trees, and the rock destroyed their legs. John checked for pulses and, finding none, went back through the cabin. The "business suit" lady was now awake and looking dazedly around.

John went to her and asked, "Can you stand up?"

She nodded and, grasping the seat-back in front of her, pulled herself erect. She grasped the briefcase as though it were her life's support, and John reached to take it while she moved out into the aisle, but she snatched it back, looking hostility at John.

"No you don't! Who are you?" It was a demand.

"I'm John Morgan. I'm the first rescuer at the site, Ma'am."

"Rescuer?" She stooped to look out the window. "Why! We're not at the airport! Where are we?" She was still disoriented.

"Your plane crashed, Ma'am, and I'm helping to get everyone out who can move. Can you walk?"

"Can't you see I'm walking? That's a sill..," and she toppled forward and into John's arms. He pried the briefcase away from her fingers and picked her up, carrying her out to the shelter area. Several able-bodied survivors were rigging a tarpaulin under one of the wide-spreading evergreens, and others were cutting and bringing in leafy branches for pallets. Some of those less mobile were already lying on these.

Pete was gently raising a man's broken leg and placing a bundle of branches under it to ease its position. He glanced up grimly at John and managed a thin grin. He'll do! John thought as he went about making a splint for the attendant's arm out of a cardboard box from among the litter.

As dawn began lightening the sky the ubiquitous TV crew arrived and began making the usual nuisances of themselves. Someone had pointed out the pair who had been first on the scene, and nothing would do but John and Pete had to drop whatever they were doing and pose for the newscasters, answering a string of unnecessary questions.

They were already out on their feet, but by now the Army medics and disaster relief people had pretty well taken over, and had the rescue of those living completed, several ambulances on their way down the treacherous road, and were bagging the bodies of the deceased.

Shortly thereafter the Army colonel had directed one of his junior officers to drive John and Pete home in one of the military vehicles, and to assign a soldier to take the horses down and stable them. "Thank God we don't have to ride back down on them!" John had remarked. He, too, was on the verge of collapse.

They hadn't been back in the house ten minutes when the phone rang. Pete answered it.

"Pete? Bob here. I saw you on the TV! Was that really you?"

"Yeah, Bob." His voice was dragging from fatigue. He wasn't up to talking, but he couldn't just cut Bob short. "Yes, we just got back to the house, and I'm pooped. I won't be in to school today. Will you tell them why?"

"OK. But what was it like?"

"Bob, I just can't talk now. I gotta crash. I'll call you later."

"Yeah, Pete, I understand. But, say! Congratulations! You did good, kid! 'Bye."

* * *

The phone rang and the soldier on watch at the house answered, "Morgan Ranch. Corporal Nelson speaking."

"Oh! May I speak with John Morgan, please?" It was Lois.

"He's asleep right now, Ma'am. They were tuckered when they got back down. I wouldn't disturb him or Mr. Milner right now, Ma'am. Could I have your name and number and have him return your call when he's up?"

"Just tell him Lois called. I'm Pete's mother."

"Oh, in that case I'd like to tell you what a fine young man you've raised. He and Mr. Morgan single-handedly took charge and guided the rescue party to the site, and then did a fine job of rendering first-aid. I wasn't up there, but I was on the radio, and I understand that if it hadn't been for their quick response and know-how, there would have been many more dead than there was. You can be justly proud of him, Ma'am. I'll tell them you called."

* * *

John had his monthly report to send in to the probation officer, and he took the opportunity to send Lois photos he'd taken of Pete around the ranch and at the airport, and one of Pete in the Cessna. There also was one of the ranch taken from the Cessna while Pete flew it. He'd been an apt student the three times they'd gone flying, and he and John were seriously talking of building a Murphy Rebel, a homebuilt kit plane. It had gotten to the stage of "we're going to build it", but not to the "when" part just yet.

In with the report and photos John had written a short letter about how well Pete was getting on. Lois' phone call after the airliner incident had been one of sheer ecstasy on her part, and John had to put the brakes on her thank-yous.

On these northern ranches where the winter weather made working on gear and tackle difficult during the seasons when not much outdoor work could be done, many had built shop buildings, where they could work on cars, trucks, tractors and other equipment, indoors, out of the weather and in relative comfort. Some were metal pre-fab, others ranged down to sheds with minimum facilities.

Uncle Gil had built a "garage," as he had called it — a concrete slab floor, wood walls and a metal roof. Another out-building was the blacksmith shop and next to it was the tack shed, both from the days when Uncle Gil's father had run larger numbers of cattle, and had had upwards of 30 draft and saddle horses to keep equipped.

With some of the money from the Buehler deal John bought insulation and drywall to close in the "garage." An old oil-stove was resurrected from the cellar, and the shop, now heated, became an ideal place to work. And it was big enough to build an airplane in!

Time out had to be taken to shop for and buy sheep and lambs preparatory to shipping the order Garry had lined up for the Fall. John had to take a couple of trips away from home, and Pete had been home alone for a night each time. At first John had had misgivings, but Pete couldn't miss school, so he did what had to be done. However, after the first trip he ceased to worry. Pete apologized for the cost of the long telephone call he'd made to his mother. He said he just forgot about the time — she was so interesting to talk to. This was a new twist, but a good one.

John had a good start on the sheep order, and there had been a healthy check of "earnest money," which helped the bank account considerably. Lois' checks had been coming in each month, and John was feeling almost foolish that he'd doubted her back when he took the chance of bankrolling her jeep's repairs.

His decision to "hire" Pete had worked out well, too. But, in Pete's weekly phone calls John had sensed that Pete was missing his mom. He never said so in so many words, but his references to her became more frequent, and his wording more of care and respect than when he'd first arrived on the ranch. John was glad for this trend. Maybe it's working.

"John, this is Lois. I have to set a date for my vacation time. I have three weeks coming and I'd like to spend some of it there on the ranch with you and Peter. I hope I'm not being too bold or presumptuous, but Peter said the other week that he'd like for me to come up there for my holiday. Would it be inconvenient?"

"Certainly not! We'd be glad if you could spend your whole vacation here. And it's about time you saw how your son is doing! You know, you've been neglecting him terribly!" Her laugh told him that she took his jibe as it was meant — in jest.

"You just give me the dates, and I'll be there to pick you up. Get most of your luggage shipped here before we pick you up — the Cessna doesn't have much cargo capacity. One ordinary bag is all you'll be allowed."

"You don't have to come to pick me up. I can drive. Or I can take the train to Kamloops."

"Nonsense! I'll get the 172, which is a 4-seater, and Pete can do most of the flying while we visit — catch up on what's been going on."

"If you insist. And, John, I showed the letter and photos to Peter's probation officer, and he seems to think everything's working out wonderfully. He says that you don't need to make such a detailed report any longer. Just a brief statement that Peter is doing well in school and hasn't developed any unpleasant habits will be sufficient."

The rest of the conversation was small talk of daily events and the cold from which she had just recovered.

"What was that all about?" Pete asked when John hung up. He had talked with his mother before she had asked to speak with John.

John told him the generalities, and the grin on Pete's face at the idea of flying his mother here with himself as pilot was like a light being turned on.

Chapter 5
An Advantageous Trade

"John, my vacation will be from the first weekend in July through the end of the month. Will that fit in with your schedule?"

"You bet it will! Remember what I told you about shipping the bulk of your luggage before we come to pick you up. And, do you have room to put both Pete and myself up overnight? Pete said he'd like me to meet his grandparents, so I figured that would be a good time to meet them."

"Yes — that's Ralph and Evelyn — they're Allan's parents, and Peter is their only grandchild. I think you'll like them, John. And, yes, I do have room: the same one you stayed in when you were here before. What would you like for dinner while you're here?"

"You fix it — I'll eat it! Remember, I got a sample of your cooking while you were my guest, and I'm still alive. How's that cold?"

"Gone. Just talking to you and Peter was the best medicine…" A few minutes more small talk and they hung up.

"What's the scoop, John?" Pete had been staying close where he could hear what was being said — at least on the one end. John gave him a review of their conversation.

Pete whooped, "You're gonna meet my Grandpa! He's cool!"

"Sounds like you approve of him."

"You betcha!" Pete crowed, picking up one of Bob's phrases. "He's a great guy!"

"What about your other grandparents — your mother's parents?"

Lois had never mentioned them, and John was curious about this family. From comments Pete had made, his father, Allan, had been "an alright guy," which could mean almost anything. From Lois' comments when she was there while the jeep was being repaired, John had gathered that Pete had been quite a tractable boy until his father had been killed.

"Mom's father died long before I was born, and her mother got married again when she was about six. She never really liked her step-father, although they got along OK, I guess. They live in Ontario. We went there once to visit them, but — I don't know — we never went back. Mom argued with him most of the time we were there, and my dad and he got into arguments. That sort of thing. She writes to her mother and my aunts sometimes, but we never see them. My two aunts came out to the funeral, but they went straight home, so I didn't get to see much of them. My dad's brother came, too, but he's living down in California, and I never see him either."

"How long ago did your dad die?" John asked. He was finally learning something about the family of this boy who was fast becoming a close friend as well as his ward.

"A little over two years ago. He worked only a few blocks from where we lived. The lady that hit him was late for work and forgot to stop at a stop sign. She was speeding — and she didn't even see him. At least, that's what she said."

"Must have been a shock. My mother died two years ago, too. But her passing was long and painful — cancer. Dad had some heart trouble, and after she passed on he sold the business and retired. I think he just quit; didn't want to live without Mom. He still lives at home, in Calgary, but he has a lady that comes in every day to clean house, fix his meals, do his laundry — things like that. He just barely hobbles around the house. I worry about him — the way he's living isn't healthy for anyone. Seems like he's just waiting to die. I tried to get him to come out here and live with me, but he won't listen."

"What did he do — work, I mean?" Pete was in a talkative mood, and John was enjoying it.

"He operated a machine shop and did gunsmithing. One of these days I'd like to get a lathe and a mill and fool around — say build up rifles, customize them, that sort of thing. Dad taught me and my brother Garry a lot about it, but nowadays there's not much money in gunsmithing — not enough to make a living on that alone. When it looked like Uncle Gil's ranch was going to be sold at auction, Dad backed my bid to buy it and keep it in the family. I never figured on being a rancher, but here I am one!"

"What did you do before you bought the ranch?"

"I worked for my dad while I was in school, and then I attended college at the University in Calgary, got a degree in Mechanical Engineering, and went to work with a small manufacturing firm in Vancouver that made marine hardware, mechanical equipment for boats and small ships. They had a long line of items, like winches and anchor fairleads and stern-tube bearings, but it was getting boring doing simple minor changes to drawings to suit some customer's whims. I was looking for a more challenging line of work when Uncle Gil died and Dad said he'd help me swing the deal.

"Funny thing: when I was working for my dad in his shop I made up my mind I didn't want to be working in a machine shop the rest of my life — lift this, thread a thousand of these studs, make two thousand nuts like this… I decided I'd get my engineering degree and get into something like designing cars or airplanes or something interesting. There I was re-designing bolt number A-752069-7A, and then doing it over again when somebody changed their mind. Now

I'm a rancher just when cattle prices are down, and this sheep thing isn't going to come around often. So the question is — what do I do with this ranch besides raise livestock on it? I'm stumped! Sure, I'll keep on with the cattle business until I can think up something else — I'd better."

Pete laughed when he looked at the expression of disgust and puzzlement on John's face, as though this was the first time he had put it all together. It was, really.

"But what else can you do on a place like this?"

"You got me there, Kiddo!" John's lopsided grin made Pete laugh. "If I knew the answer to that one, I'd be doing it."

*　　*　　*

The book of plans and instructions for the Rebel had arrived. Pete had opened the package before John got home from a trip to Kamloops, and had the many papers and drawings spread out, and was hopping from one to another. One of the first things they needed to build was a 16 foot long table that was absolutely level and would form the base of all construction of the airplane's components. John had already acquired the two sheets of plywood for the top, and timbers for the legs and bracings. The newly spruced-up shop was soon going to see plenty of activity!

Since they had placed the order for the Rebel kit the Morgan Ranch shop building had become a sort of Mecca for many of Pete's school friends. Factory photos and drawings of the Rebel papered the walls, and a solid work-bench had been built along one wall.

The 4 by 16 foot table for the jig was taking shape in the middle of the floor.

Of course the routine work of keeping the ranch operating took precedence, and Bob had been hired on a part-time basis to help when sheep were arriving from John's purchases. The Arab deal was working out better than John had expected, and with the buyer taking care of the shipping to Seattle, much of the cost and worry was not on John's shoulders.

The Buehler cattle were sold and the "compound" cleared for more sheep. They already had over half the mature sheep and most of the lambs they needed for the Fall shipment. To top that off, John's prices for the sheep were below what he'd estimated, which meant even more profit. Another "earnest-money" check had arrived, which was welcome. With the weather now smoothing out, John was using one or the other of the Cessnas to do his "sheep-dealing" trips, but, as most of these were when Pete was in school, the trips were solo.

A Luscombe had become available for rental at the airport, and John got himself checked out in it. It was very close to the Rebel in configuration and performance, and being a tail-dragger, it would provide invaluable experience against the day when he would be test-flying the Rebel. That was quite a while in the future, but the more experience "in type" he could get, the better. The Luscombe had a Continental 85 hp engine, but the characteristics were similar to the Murphy with a hundred or so horses. The wing section, being very similar, would be the best teacher. The Luscombe was a NACA4412 section and the Murphy was a 4415, which was a slightly thicker section, but with similar flight characteristics.

* * *

The phone rang and Pete answered. It was Bob. "Hey, Pete! I just picked up this awesome video with Tom Selleck in it, called Quigley Down Under. It's a Western about an American sharp-shooter in Australia, an' there's this outrageous rifle he's got. Ya just gotta see it!

"You bet I do. Wait a minute, let's see if John wants to see it too." He called to John, in the other room, and explained the offer.

"Count me in. Tonight?" Pete relayed the message. It was set; Bob would bring it over that evening.

After the movie, over chips and dip, they discussed the flick.

"Didja ever see such rad shootin'?" Pete exclaimed.

"Well, those old rifles packed quite a wallop at long range," John replied, "and I'm quite willing to believe that a 500 grain slug from a 45-110 Sharps would flip that heavy bucket end over end at, say, 5, 6 or even 700 yards. As for a man making such an offhand shot that quickly, and after setting his sights so casually as old Quigley appeared to be doing, well — that's the difference between the movies and real life."

Pete sat silent for a few minutes, then asked, "Could I get a rifle like that?"

"Well, you can get anything you want, if you can pay for it, Pete. Why? Would you like to have a rifle like that?"

"Yeah, I would! That'd be bad! I mean, who else would have one like that? Bob Jennings has a .270 and Larry Weldon has a .30-30 — at least his dad lets him use it, but it ain't really his own rifle."

Bob remarked. "I have that old Winchester 1886 in .45-70 that Dad gave me for my 16th birthday, but it won't hit anything at that distance,"

"How much would a rifle like that cost?" Pete asked.

John shrugged, "Maybe $15-18 hundred U.S. Lotta bucks."

Pete lapsed into silence. Might as well be a million, he thought to himself. Bob said he had to go, as it was a school day tomorrow, and they all said their good-byes.

John said, "When we go to Kamloops on the weekend let's stop in at Libinatti's Sporting Goods shop and see what we see there. He often has some unusual rifles in stock."

Pete's tone, more than his words, betrayed his morose view of the matter: "Not much point in lookin', if it's going to cost that much."

"Well, we can always look. Say, have you decided what you're gonna make for your wood shop project yet?"

"No, I haven't. The teacher suggested making a bedside table, but I don't need one."

"What about your mom? Could she use one? I'll bet she'd be proud as all get-out if you made one for her."

"Nah. She's got a complete bedroom suite. Anything I could make wouldn't look right."

"Any other ideas?"

"Yeah, I got one. Ya know that stool over in the blacksmith shop?"

"The one my grandpa made."

"Do you suppose I could make one like that? I mean — I think it would be neat!"

"I don't see why you couldn't. Uncle Gil always said it looked like it came out of a Viking ship — although I don't suppose they had stools on those longboats of theirs."

Actually, Uncle Gil had said it looked like it came out of a Viking brothel, but John decided a little editing wouldn't spoil the general sentiment.

"Why don't you go over to the shop after supper, dust it off, bring it over to the house, and make a detailed drawing of it?"

After supper Pete brought the stool into the kitchen and tried to get it to stand up, but the broken leg wouldn't hold at all.

"Could we glue it?" Pete asked.

"Well, we could, but why bother? Just let it lay there on the floor and make some drawings from it."

Pete looked puzzled, "What'll I draw? Where do I start?"

"If you're going to make a duplicate of it — or a near duplicate — you need to make good new parts exactly like every good part in that stool. Get yourself a pencil and eraser and some paper, and start studying how it's put together. You're going to have to really look at every part of that stool, Pete."

Pete didn't look very enthusiastic. "You can't just look at it and make drawings of the parts, John," he said.

"I didn't say to just look at it, Peter. I said to really look at it. Could you draw a freehand map of New Zealand?"

"Well…ah…no. Probably not a good one. It's west of Australia, isn't it?" Pete said, looking further confused.

John laughed. "Well, your first problem would be to find it on a map, I guess. But let's say you dug out the atlas and traced the map of New Zealand, then maybe drew in the latitudes and longitudes, and then located maybe 10 major cities on your drawing. Then you printed their names in as neatly as you could. Afterwards do you think you could draw a better freehand map of New Zealand than you could before?"

"Yes, I guess so…"

"OK, why?"

Pete grinned, "Because tracing it out real careful would have made me really pay attention to the details."

"Exactly! Now, apply the same degree of attention to every piece of that stool, and you'll have it in the bag in an hour or so."

Pretty soon Pete was down on the floor on his hands and knees beside the old stool, with a paper and pencil, and was applying a ruler to every nook and cranny of the stool. At one point he exclaimed, "Wow! Ain't that neat!" John pretended he hadn't heard and kept his attention on some work of his own.

"Hey, John. Come and look at this. Your grandfather musta been a really smart guy. Look how these two pieces interlock! And, you know — I think I know how this leg got busted. I think it got kicked by a horse! You see here? There's half a horseshoe print here by the broke off piece."

John came over and hunkered down on the balls of his feet beside Pete to look.

"You're quite the detective, aren't you? I was about your age, helping Uncle Gil shoe old Bud, when that stool got busted. Bud was a real quiet workhorse we had back then — back about 1963, it would have been. He was just standing there, quiet, with his foot just about done, when Tippy — that was a dog we had here then — came tearing through the blacksmith shop and out right under old Bud's feet. I think he was after a cat. Well, old Bud was so startled he just about exploded! He kicked that stool about 30 yards across the barnyard. I'd completely forgotten about that incident until you found that horseshoe print. What were you saying about an interlocked joint?"

Pete showed him. "You see, it's so simple you wouldn't really notice it at first, but when you do you realize that yer grandpa must have been one smart dude."

John tousled Pete's hair as he stood up. "That he was, Pete, that he was." John recalled something from when he had been perhaps five years old. His grandfather had been showing him how to tie a knot, when his older brother had horned in on the proceedings.

"Now you just go on about your own affairs, Garry. I'm showing John something right now." It was the first time in his short life that any adult had put him ahead of his older brother.

From that moment on, Grampa walked on water so far as John was concerned.

"How can I get the right shape for the leg profile?" Pete finally asked.

"Just draw what you see," John told him.

Pete looked puzzled.

"OK, look. You know the top and bottom of the legs are parallel: the bottom of the seat is parallel with the floor, and the bottoms of the legs are parallel with the floor. You now have two parallel lines a measurable distance apart. Lay out two parallel lines about six or eight inches apart on your paper. Then draw in the shape of the leg between those lines as you see it. But, you want to look at every inch of that curve as closely as you would if you were looking for a single splinter which, if you only had one chance at it, and if you pushed it the right direction, would dump $5,000 in gold coins in your lap."

Some while later Pete looked up as though emerging from a trance.

"What time is it? Were you talking to me?"

John pointed to the clock on the kitchen wall and shook his head. "Nope. I never said a word. How's your drawing coming?"

"Well, I think I have something here that is pretty close — and if it isn't, it's just as good." He brought it over to show John, who looked at it critically for a couple of minutes. Shifting his gaze to the stool and back he said, "I agree, if it ain't identical, it's as good as the original."

"Now what?" Pete asked.

"Well, you'll need to work up a full size layout. Have you ever had to enlarge a drawing by means of a grid?"

"You mean like where each square represents a bigger square? Like in a book where it has 1/8" squares that equal 2" squares in real life?"

"That's right. You figure out how big it is in your little drawing and how big it has to be in real life — and you're on your way. You're going to need a bigger piece of paper. Why not cut open a big grocery bag from the drawer over there."

Half an hour later Pete began cutting out a leg pattern and trying it against the leg of the old stool.

"How's she fit?" John asked.

Pete stood back and looked at the results of about 2-1/2 hours of intense mental concentration and finally said, "You know, I don't think it's off more than a quarter of an inch anywhere! Man, that is so cool!"

Peter's stool was to be more of a success than he could have imagined. That Saturday they went to Kamloops and looked in at Libinatti's Sporting Goods store. After talking with John and Pete for a while, the proprietor excused himself and made a phone call. Returning, he told them a friend had a Shiloh Sharps which she was interested in selling. She was asking $1,400 for it.

"That's a good price for it, too. I've seen it," Libinatti added.

Back in the Land Cruiser Pete said, "I don't want to go see it, John. Where would I ever get 1,400 bucks?" His voice reflected his dejection.

"Well, it never hurts to look," John replied. "If Libinatti says it's a good price, it is. You can bet on it."

They found the address, a small roadside cafe, and the person to speak with turned out to be a small, middle aged, rotund lady. She was pleasant enough, and showed them the rifle, saying she had inherited it along with a lot of other things from an uncle. After they had eaten and paid for a pair of sandwiches and were outside again, John stopped Pete and asked, "Pete, what's wrong with the seating in there?"

Pete gave him a puzzled look.

"Think about what they have for seating at the counter."

"Just some chairs. But they're way too low. They're uncomfortable. Why?"

"How would your stool do in there?"

"Hey! I see what you mean! Maybe I could get her to trade the rifle for a bunch of stools."

"Now you're getting my drift! Finish the one you're making before you go running in there, and then show her the sample. Get an order, and it just might work out. That rifle — she's asking $1,400 for it — but did you see the dust on it? There haven't been any potential buyers flocking to look at it. She just might be more amenable to dickering after she sees your stool. How many stools do you think she could use?

"More'n a dozen. Let's do it!"

"I'd guess maybe 16. I was countin' spaces."

Some weeks later Pete rubbed the final coat of oil into the last of 16 stools and they were on their way to complete the trade. Pete caressed his "Quigley" rifle all the way home.

Chapter 6
A Woman's Touch

The flight to Vancouver was uneventful. The 172 was properly greased onto the runway and duly fueled, then tied down at the Transient Ramp. Lois had spied the green and white 172 when they were at the gas pumps, and came out to greet them. After giving Pete a bear hug she stopped just short of doing the same to John, and he found he regretted that she didn't. She was bubbling over with excitement, and John did a double-take; was this the thirty six year old mother of this teenager? The lady with troubled eyes? Or was she a school-girl on her first outing? Her eyes flashed and her chestnut hair blew free in the steady breeze. Her eyes had lost that worried look and she seemed a different person. He liked what he saw.

They went first to "Grandpa and Grandma Milner's." John admitted to himself he'd had some trepidation about meeting Lois' husband's parents. Not that he had any thoughts about her, of course.

Pete's grandparents turned out to be two rather thoughtful and pleasant oldsters. Right away the senior Milner said, "I'm Ralph and she's Evelyn. We don't stand much on ceremony. And you're the John I've been hearing so much about." He extended a paw whose grip made John wince. This man used his hands! They were hard-skinned and muscled.

Evelyn was almost as tall as her husband, her thick white hair drawn back neatly, with a hint of Italian ancestry to her features and eyes. She confirmed that by promptly suggesting a repast she had prepared. It was about that time, and they were all ready!

After the small talk during the meal Pete said, "Grandpa, whyn't you show John what you have in your 'grarge,'" mimicking Ralph's pronunciation.

The three men retired to the double garage behind the house. As Ralph swung the door open it revealed a bench along one side with a big husky old flat-belt South Bend 11 by 36" lathe with sleeve bearings, and beyond that an old Bridgeport mill.

"This is my 'Toy Shop' and 'Sand-Box,' where I come to play. Know anything about this stuff?"

"Some. My dad owned a machine shop and gunsmithing business up until a couple years ago, and I worked for him summers and weekends and holidays, in between going to work for my Uncle Gil on the ranch. One of these days I'm going to get a lathe and mill and just play with them — make just anything that tickles my fancy. I still take Home Shop Machinist and Live Steam and that other one — Projects in Metal. I still like looking at that stuff, but I don't have the time to do anything about it right now."

John looked with longing at the machines, and as his eyes roamed, he saw a dividing head, milling cutters, grinders and the many things that go to make up a complete machine shop suitable for a toolmaker. He reached out and ran his hands over the machinery — a caress. The polished steel felt familiar and friendly.

Ralph saw the question in John's eyes, and responded, "My brother Joe and I — we had a shop up in Edmonton. Did fairly well until Joe died about ten years ago. I retired and sold off everything except the machinery. The buyer was buying just the property and dealership we had; the machine shop end was in support of the farming equipment we represented as dealers — plus a little walk-in trade. Anyhow, this is what remains of the equipment. I come out here to stay out of Evelyn's hair, and make things like this dividing head and some other things, just for the fun of it. Sounds silly, I guess, but I enjoy it."

Ralph had handed John a small version of a machinist's dividing head, a tool that holds the workpiece in either a lathe-type chuck or a pair of lathe centers and can rotate it and lock it into any position, dividing the circumference of any circle into as many divisions as the user desires, for drilling, milling or any other machining operation.

"This is beautiful!" John exclaimed, turning it over and looking at it from every angle. He'd give his eye teeth for one like it. He wandered from machine to machine, fondling them as though they were alive. Ralph followed him, enjoying seeing a kindred spirit appreciating fine machinery.

Back in the house Lois reminded him they had things to do if they were leaving in the morning. Taking leave of the senior Milners, they drove to her home, and the evening was spent selecting what she'd take in the morning. The trunk with her spare clothes had been shipped that morning and was well on its way.

*　*　*

"Hold it! You haven't set your trim." Pete's face reddened as he pushed the toggle and watched the indicator move to ten degrees. John checked and said, "OK — let 'er rip!"

Pete smoothly advanced the throttle knob to full open and the Cessna responded by gently pushing the three of them into their seat-backs as it accelerated down the runway. There was a slight right quartering wind, and Pete dipped the right wing into it and held straight ahead as the wheels quit rumbling and the plane lifted smoothly into the air. The climb-out was normal, and John picked up the mike, saying into it, "Cessna Coca November departing eastward, VFR to Kamloops."

The speaker crackled, "Cessna Coca November, have a nice trip."

They did. Pete was king! John left him alone and he climbed out to 6500 feet altitude, leveled off and set up a course of 040 degrees, magnetic. With the slight wind reported, they should hit the airport at Kamloops right on the button. The sky was a clear blue and the morning was warm. John had gone over the flight plan with him before they had fired up the bird, and Pete had it right the first time.

Lois took all this in, missing nothing. She noted Pete's head swinging right to left and back again as he scanned the sky for other aircraft. Ten minutes into the flight he calmly noted, "Aircraft, one o'clock, high," followed shortly by, "He'll pass over us in about three minutes."

John grinned at Lois. He'd refrained from conversation to let Pete show her his competence. He was doing superbly. John left him at the controls, although from the right seat, until Kamloops was well within sight.

"Turn to about course six-oh. That'll bring her closer to the pattern."

He picked up the mike and called Kamloops tower, "Kamloops, Cessna Coca November, for a landing, inbound from Vancouver. Give me your wind and traffic, please."

The speaker crackled. "Cessna Coca November, wind calm, Temperature twenty five Centigrade. Altimeter, two-niner point niner eight. Cleared to land." This told John there were no other aircraft approaching or in the traffic area.

"Pete, set up our pattern entry, eight hundred AGL and I'll take over when you're ready."

The Cessna made a professional entry into the traffic pattern, and on downwind Pete said, "OK, it's all yours".

"What's AGL mean?" Lois asked.

"Above Ground Level. The ground elevation is given on the charts for each airport. The normal traffic pattern altitude is 800 feet." John took over the controls for the actual landing.

Jerry wandered out from his office as they fueled up the bird and John went to get his station wagon and bring it around. Pete was finishing the fueling and introduced Jerry to his mother.

"You've got a fine son here. Did he fly you here from Vancouver?"

"Yes. And he did a beautiful job of it. Better than any airliner I've ridden in." She radiated pride. John arrived with the wagon, and the small amount of luggage was transferred.

*   *   *

Lois was bubbling over with questions on the ride to the ranch. What all was Pete doing in school? What were his friends like? Would she get to meet this Bob he had spoken about on the phone several times? What kind of work had he been doing at the ranch?

He had told her about most of these things on the phone and in letters, but she was here now and these questions were again fresh — she was about to see and meet the people and things that made up her son's life.

John said not a word, simply enjoying hearing the excitement in her voice and watching the expressions play on her face. She is a lovely woman! I've never noticed before. Why? Her eyes sparkled and danced.

Settling in at the house occupied part of the afternoon, and then John took her for a tour of the ranch. Pete was on the phone with Bob, telling about the trip and his flying it both ways. When Lois had been here before, she hadn't seen all of the house, as John had parts of it closed off to conserve heating; now he gave her a tour of the house first.

Like most ranch houses in the area, it was two-story, with five bedrooms upstairs and three baths. She had seen the two they had stayed in and John's when she cleaned house a couple of times, but the other rooms had been closed.

Then John showed her the cellar, with its large walk-in freezer and seemingly yards and yards of shelves loaded with vegetable and fruit preserves. He picked up a large jar of sauerkraut, saying, "My Aunt Bertie made the best sauerkraut you've ever tasted. She was German, and after the war Uncle Gil served in the Occupation, and met her. She was the best cook I ever knew. A wonderful woman. When I was little, Mom and Dad sent me to spend a few weeks with them every vacation, and she made over me so I almost hated going home. I liked playing with my cousins Jack and Harry, but they're gone now. They were a few years older than me, but they taught me how to ride and rope and do all the things a rancher needs to know. After they went to college I worked here during summers when Dad didn't need me in the shop."

"How do you mean your cousins are gone?" Lois asked.

"They were both killed in an airline crash in Java. They had formed a company after college and were speculating in foreign oil properties. Never found out just what really happened to the plane. That was quite a few years ago. Broke Uncle Gil's and Aunt Bertie's heart. She didn't live long after that, and Uncle Gil went downhill too."

They were now outside and he gave Lois the tour of their new shop, showing her the table for the airplane jig, and describing where the machine-shop portion was going to be — sometime in the future.

"I wish I had the money now. I'd like to teach Pete machine-work and gunsmithing. He'd eat it up!"

The tour continued out into the fields and he showed her the pipeline Pete had run to the compound when the Buehler cattle were there. After that, he showed her the other recent developments they'd made.

"Pete's shaping up to be whatever he chooses to be. He learns fast, and he remembers. How'd you like the way he planned and executed that flight?" It was more of a statement. She said nothing, but was thinking, It's impossible that there has been so much change in Peter in this short amount of time.

As John headed for the house with the last light of day, Lois covertly studied this quiet, self-assured man that had made her disasters turn into pleasures, and realized her thoughts about him had been only about what appeared on the surface — superficial. Now she was seeing the deeper man.

*   *   *

Two large but not heavy cardboard boxes arrived and were eagerly opened after the day's work was completed. The contents consisted of large formed aluminum parts, stamped and with rivet holes punched. Among the remaining items were a rivet puller and bags of pull-type rivets, similar to the familiar pop-rivets, but stressed for aircraft use. The late afternoon and after dinner were consumed with three pair of eyes looking over the plans and parts, determining which part went with what other, and the sequence of riveting to prevent painting themselves into a corner.

The next morning, work schedules were studied to see if some afternoon hours could be pirated to get a start on assembly of the bird. Eager hands were itching to see parts mature into assembled components, and, although they knew better, they each felt that every minute counted. They were to learn that the old proverb, "Haste makes waste" was not an idle saying.

The first kit was for the empennage — "tail feathers" in aviation parlance — and eagerly parts were matched up, rivets inserted in holes and "pulled."

Two hours into this exciting activity they found that the top and bottom skins for the horizontal stabilizer were nicely riveted together along their joining seam, but now it was impossible to get the internal stiffener into it and align holes to rivet it in place.

Reluctantly, the rivets so happily pulled were drilled out and the parts separated so the internal structural elements could be located first. Fortunately John had been able to acquire a coffee can full of "Cleco Fasteners", temporary clamping devices that fit in the holes to hold the parts together while doing the fit-up and early riveting, and these soon solved the problem. But other problems were in the offing.

This was a common failing with new builders, and the kit had included a few dozen extra rivets in anticipation of the problem.

The next evening the builders were more circumspect, and by the end of the second evening one completed stabilizer was lying on the table. After the first night of trying to position the polished aluminum parts on a harsh wooden surface with tiny metal drill-chips trying to mar the finish, John had pirated a throw rug from one of the unused bedrooms, and the parts were cushioned while being assembled. John finished the evening by diligently polishing out some early scratches, and decided to buy some cheap carpeting to cover the table on his next trip to Kamloops.

*   *   *

With all the work of upgrading the ranch for the regularly incoming sheep and lambs, John hadn't noticed, but Lois had been quietly upgrading the interior of the house. There hadn't been a woman's touch here since Aunt Bertie had died, and Lois was busy remedying that.

The first thing noticed by a woman are the curtains. They were old and faded. This was her first project.

Borrowing the station wagon, she drove into Kamloops and bought yardage of several patterns. She had discovered Aunt Bertie's well-stocked sewing kit, and had made plans.

By the end of the first week John was beginning to notice each room in the living part of the house was — for some reason he couldn't put his finger on — looking brighter and more cheerful. It wasn't until he discovered the new curtains in his own bedroom that he realized what the difference was.

"Where did you get the new curtains?" he asked Lois at the dinner table.

"I made them. Do you like them?" she said with a pleased smile. It was then that the realization dawned on him that this was the root of the difference he had noted, but couldn't place.

"They're great!" he exclaimed, looking into her eyes across the table. "Thank you, Lois," he said with an unaccountable catch in his throat, "I'd never noticed how shabby the curtains had become, and it took a few double-takes to realize what had been changing. Thank you very much."

"You're very welcome," she smiled back, her eyes shining. "After all, look at what you've done for us, rescuing us from the blizzard, and getting the jeep fixed, and what you've done for Peter..." Her eyes were now glistening around the edges with moisture.

John began feeling uncomfortable with all this sentiment, and quickly changed the subject. "Jerry has a new Oshkosh video. Says we can borrow it the next time we're in Kamloops."

"Yeah — can we do that?!" Pete said.

"Yeah, I guess so," John replied absently.

Pete looked from his mother to John and back again. He was puzzled about something going on that he didn't understand.

John had just had another attack of Dorie-itis. He pictured the idyllic first few days with Dorie, and the aftermath of a spoiled child when she learned that his money wasn't unlimited. Once burned...

Lois didn't understand the sudden withdrawal of his happy demeanor either, and was more puzzled than hurt. Things at the table were quiet for several minutes until gradually the small talk of ranch things resumed, and the moment was lost. John had crawled back into the protective shell of work. Lois, with a woman's perceptivity, had figured out his problem, and had backed off.

*　*　*

On one of their earlier horseback trips Lois had noticed the pair of large binoculars John had brought along, and was amazed at the distances they could tame. She was using them now to look from their picnic spot on a ridge across the valley to the opposite hillside, where she could clearly see a deer grazing placidly.

"John, I've never seen glasses as good as these. Where are they made?"

"Japan. They're 16 by 70 Fujinons. That means they bring things in 16 times closer, and the big objective lenses up front are 70 millimeters — or about 2-3/4" — across, which is what gives them such tremendous light gathering power. Among other things, they're completely waterproof, which makes them very easy to clean. I'd think nothing of washing them off in a river or lake, if the water was clean. You'd want to pat the water off the lenses afterwards of course, or you could have trouble from etching or minerals being left on the lens surfaces, but otherwise, it wouldn't hurt them at all."

"They must have cost a fortune!"

"Well, not exactly. Actually, they were given to me. A year or so before I bought the ranch I did a favor for a friend who had a steel fabricating business. He built things — special buildings, tank support frames and things like that — and he'd bought a building to expand into. He had been using overhead bridge cranes to move the heavy loads, but this new building he'd bought wasn't sturdy enough for overhead cranes, and he was faced with a huge expense to reinforce the structure for them.

"I suggested he build a couple of rubber-tired mobile straddle cranes to handle the work. He asked me to draw up a conceptual design for something like that, so I did. I designed them so he could use them singly or together, depending on the load to be handled. He built them in his own shop with his crew, and they proved to be so versatile that he figured they saved him several hundred thousand dollars. When I gave him my drawings he was so pleased he gave me these binoculars, as a gift. After a while — in fact, just about the time he got around to figuring out how much the cranes had saved him — he got an order from a customer for six more just like them. About a month after the last of those were delivered and paid for, I received a letter, along with a check for a goodly amount.

"I didn't want to accept it, as I hadn't done that much work, but he insisted, saying my idea and design work had put many times the amount of the check into his pocket. That — along with the money from Dad — is what I used to buy the ranch when it went on the block."

"That's a wonderful story!" Lois exclaimed. "A person never knows what good deed will come back many-fold. I think it says something like that in the Bible, doesn't it?"

* * *

There were a couple more weekend trips to beautiful secluded mountain glades for picnic lunches and fishing at streams that seemed to be hundreds of miles from any civilization. Then the vacation drew to a close. The "spare clothes" trunk was shipped, and the three loaded up the 172 and Pete made another creditable take-off and flight. This time John didn't take over until Pete had turned on final approach into Langley Airport.

The Cessna was fueled and Pete and John were saying their good-byes. As John was about to turn to walk to the Cessna, Lois stepped closer and stood on tiptoes to give him a kiss. Before he realized it, his arms were around her and he was responding fully. It felt so good to have a woman's kiss, one with the edge of passion to it. They broke apart and he stepped back slightly, still leery of the feelings.

"Thank you, John, for all you've done for us. Peter is a different boy, and I'm so proud of him now. And, it's all your fault!" She told her real meaning by her small, deprecating smile as she stepped away.

* * *

Summer passed into early Fall, and the sheep and lambs were being loaded into cattle transport trucks for shipment to Seattle. That was one full week of heat and dust, from daylight to dark, and Red and Mouse were wet and dog-tired when they were rubbed down and put away each night. The dusty and sweaty pair of riders showered, fixed the simplest meal they could think of, and turned in. Pete didn't even call his mother that week. They were too tired to talk, and the meals were eaten in silence, except for requests to pass something. Bob had been on the payroll, too, but there was plenty of work to go around.

When that week was over John had time to think again. Memories of Lois' summer visit were frequent, and John enjoyed recalling them. In the evenings he and Lois had often talked idly about their lives and work. He had described growing up helping his dad in the machine shop, and the days working with his uncle and cousins on the ranch, then about his work with the marine hardware business and his boredom over designing part number C-24763 over and over again. He had covered much of what he and Pete had discussed, and his dilemma about what he was going to do with the ranch after the sheep were gone what with the depressed cattle business. There didn't seem to be a viable answer.

Lois was a computer medical transcriber at a major hospital, and liked the work. The pay wasn't all that good, but was enough for her to make do with. Allan had been an accountant and she had helped him with some "moonlighting" with tax preparations. She liked working with computers. But, that held her to the city, and she was getting to like the open spaces. She liked seeing mountains on the horizon.

One day she and John had ridden to the site of the airplane crash, and she had marveled at John's description of the way Pete had performed when the chips were down. Pete was in school for some make-up work he had missed at the beginning, and it was a time for just the two of them.

"The nose was here, and the plane was pointed that way. You can see the gash it made through the trees, but at least they were softer than the bare rocks for their initial impact. That probably saved several lives."

"You said Peter was a big help in the first hours after the two of you got here that night. What did he do?"

"Well, as soon as we reached the site and saw the situation, I got on the radio and called in the location. Pete went to get the first aid kit and blankets, and then we went into the airplane to see how many were still alive. Pete helped with identifying the injured and helped some get outside. Then he helped set up the shelter under the trees."

"This was his first time to see anything that terrible. Wasn't he upset?"

"Yes. When he entered the plane and saw a dead man, he turned and threw up, but right away he was back to give me a hand. I showed him how to mark those who were alive but unable to help themselves, so the rescuers could get aid to them more quickly. He's a good, steady man in an emergency."

"You said 'man.' Isn't he awfully young to class as a man?"

"I don't look at years. Out here we judge a person by what they do. He's been doing a man's work. He accepts responsibility. He has shown me that he's a man. Young, maybe, but a man for all that."

Later they rode to the repeater station and the view from there was breathtaking. To the north was Bonaparte Lake, and far to the east were the ridges of the Rockies; to the west there were those of the Cadwellder Range. She had fixed some fried chicken and potato salad, two of his favorites, and they sat and had a picnic while he named off the points in the distance.

He had felt a camaraderie with her in this easy private companionship and wished she didn't have to go back to the city.

But life had to go on; she had a job to return to and he… Well, he didn't let himself think beyond that point. Once burnt…

There was one thing that stayed in the back of his mind through the hot, dusty days of the sheep loading. There had been plenty of time to think. She had made an observation when talking about a friend who had been widowed, and later found a new mate, which kept coming back to his mind.

She had said, "Jane's marriage to Don was beautiful. They weren't just husband and wife, they were best friends. Constant companions. When Don died — of an aneurysm — she remembered the beauty of her marriage, and when she met Alex she wasn't afraid to remarry. I guess those who have had good marriages that are interrupted by death or other cause are less afraid to enter into it again. When they find the right one, of course."

Was his own problem the obverse of that? Did his failed marriage to Dorie blind him to what it could be? Lois had apparently had an ideal marriage to Allan — similar to what she described Jane as having had with Don. But it's such a big gamble! And I've never been successful at gambling — the few times I've tried.

Chapter 7
Free to Go

The tail feathers of the Rebel were beginning to look like airplane parts when another pair of large boxes appeared. These were long and skinny, and when opened, revealed the formed aluminum parts for the wing. Once again the plans were spread on every horizontal surface in the house, and parts compared with drawings. This was going to take them well into the winter!

There had been more glitches in the tail feathers of course. One of the internal stiffeners had been originally installed upside down, and riveted. Drilling the rivets back out left the holes oversize and John decided to send for a new part instead of trying to mickey-mouse it. Pete had said, "Why? Nobody'll ever see those holes!"

"Maybe not. But I'll know they're not right. That's gonna be my butt up there in this bird, and I don't want to start worrying if maybe I should have done it right. Probably nothing would happen — there's no great stress on that joint — but I'd rather do it right than worry about it."

Pete thought that over in silence for a while.

*   *   *

Hunting season interfered with airplane building. John bought Pete an Enfield that a friend in Kamloops had put up for sale. Pete had fired the "Quigley," as they dubbed it, and the recoil was extreme, particularly to a young buck not used to heavy-caliber shooting.

The new Enfield was a Remington-built P-17, the English-designed, American-built rifle of World War I. The British government had been experimenting with a .280 Magnum design in 1914, when the war broke out. They contracted with the American firms of Remington and Winchester to build these rifles, but in British .303 caliber, since they needed rifles immediately, and didn't have time to complete development of the .280. The Enfield arsenal and other contractors were already at peak production of the Short, Magazine, Lee Enfield rifles, commonly known as the SMLE.

When the U.S. entered the war in 1917, they needed all the production they could get, and modified this Enfield design to take the .30-06 cartridge. These were called the P-17, for Pattern of 1917. Production was revived when World War II broke out, but this time the production went to the U.S. until production of the M-1 Garand got into full swing.

The P-17 John bought had been converted to a sporter by milling the top rear of the receiver round to match the front receiver ring, putting it in a sporter stock of beautifully-grained walnut, and mounting a 6-power scope on it. It was good enough for the largest game in North America, and Pete went into orbit when John gave it to him on his 17th birthday.

"Technically, by law, you can't own a firearm until you're 18," John said, "So as far as this goes, it's my rifle for the next year, but it's yours to use and take care of. On your 18th birthday it's legally all yours."

Pete was speechless. He turned it this way and that. He pulled out the bolt and sighted through the barrel, commenting that it had 4-groove rifling — they were made in both 2- and 4-groove, and although there was no difference in shooting characteristics, the relative merit of the two types of rifling was the subject of many debates among riflemen.

"Thanks," was all he could get out for some time, and then he looked long at John and said, "After all the trouble I've been to you…" There was a question there.

"Trouble? What trouble? You've helped me get the ranch in shape to take on the work I was able to get; Buehler first and then the sheep deal. You helped me make up my mind on the Rebel — I don't think I'd have dared to take it on without knowing I'd have your help with it. And, it was pretty lonesome out here before I brought you here to help me. I think everything's worked out pretty well for both of us."

Pete looked at John for several long seconds, and John could see that he was fighting back tears — obviously this was a much larger compliment than he'd ever had before.

*　　*　　*

The next Saturday when Pete called his mother he told her all about the present. She did a mental double-take, and then asked to talk to John after they'd finished.

"John, don't think I don't appreciate your gift to Pete, but isn't it playing with fire to give a gun to someone as young as Pete, especially with his trouble — and immaturity?" She had seen the Sharps, but thought it was really John's rifle, and neither of them had made any attempt at clarification of that point. As with the Enfield, technically, the Shiloh Sharps rifle was John's.

"I don't see any immaturity in him any longer, Lois. He's grown into a responsible young man, no longer the insecure boy that lived in Vancouver. He's discovered manhood, and I'd trust him with my life any time, now. He had the right stuff, but just never had a chance to see what he really could do. I saw him in action at the crash. That was the first time in his life he'd seen sudden, shocking, gruesome death and injury — and he buckled down and did what any competent man would do — in fact, better than many full-grown men I know. He acted like a man. I've hunted with him. We've sat and talked, many times — long into the night. We've studied navigation together, and principles of flight. He's helped me working on the tractors and other farm equipment, and the airplane — he's a good mechanic.

"I've flown with him, and as I see him, he'll make a 'natural' pilot. To be a good pilot you have to have confidence in yourself and your own judgment — and he has that. You've seen it. Don't you think that I've had much more opportunity lately to judge his real character than you — or anyone else — has had?"

"Ye-es," she said grudgingly, as she thought over this radically new — to her — concept. She was still thinking about his failures and attempts to emulate the Shugard boys.

"Yes, I can see the changes. It's just hard for me to realize and believe what I've seen this past summer. You've done wonders with him, John. Someday I'll think of some way to repay you for all you've done for him."

Jokingly he replied, "Oh, I'll think of a way, someday." Some small talk followed and ended the conversation, and they hung up.

His final statement haunted John as he lay in bed before falling asleep that night. Turning his words over he could see many meanings. It could be taken as an invitation for intimacies — as payment! This had not been his intent. He had been momentarily unprepared for the situation, and said what popped into his mind. Foot-in-mouth-disease, he thought.

It could also be taken as a half-hearted proposal of marriage — for some time in the future. The thought of marriage still made him break out in a sweat. Of course, Lois was an entirely different kind of woman from Dorie. Hope I haven't opened a Pandora's box with my offhand comment! Sleep ended further conjecture.

*   *   *

On one of his supply trips into Kamloops during the week, when Pete was in school, and he had to transact some business with the bank, John had lunch at a familiar diner. He recognized Larry Wilkes, the General Manager of the Kamloops Memorial Hospital, sitting alone at a table. Larry was another EAA member. His lunch hadn't arrived and he waved for John to join him. John accepted, and the two made small-talk, including some "hangar-flying."

As casual conversations often will, it drifted toward business problems, and Larry said, "I've got one that's bugging me! As you might imagine, all hospital records are kept in excruciating detail. My transcriber is getting married and leaving me. I had one hell of a time getting her in the first place — two years ago."

"Are they that hard to find?"

"Yes. Out here, particularly. I had to pay moving costs to get her to come here from Calgary. It's all computer now, you know, and really good computer people are hard to find — they're all in the big cities — Vancouver, Edmonton, Calgary — you name it. But not here."

"Larry, you've met Pete, the young man staying with me — working for me. His mother is a Medical Transcriber in Vancouver. She hates to be separated from him, but I need him, and he's here to be away from some rather obnoxious people there. Would you be interested in maybe talking to Pete's mother?"

"You can bet I would! When?"

"Whoah! I don't know if she'd be interested. It's a long drive in from the ranch to Kamloops, and I know if she were to move here she'd want to be at the ranch to be near Pete."

"That's no problem. You got a computer?"

"No. Why?"

"All this transcribing nowadays is by computer. She wouldn't have to leave the house. Get a computer with a modem in it. I can send the audio tapes by phone and she can transcribe them, and send them here by the modem. You know what I'm talking about?"

"Yes — in general. I've used computers, but I don't have one. Not now, anyway."

"Tell you what. You get on the phone with your lady-friend and see if the idea interests her. If it does, I'll furnish the computer and any needed equipment. John, I need a transcriber yesterday!"

Larry fished a card out of his wallet, and handed it to John. "Here's my phone. At home and the hospital. Have her call me — any decent hour of the day or night. I've had three applicants, but none of them has any medical transcription experience. This kind of work is not something you can learn on-the-job!"

On his way back out to the ranch his mind mulled over Larry's reference to, "…your lady-friend…" He'd made it clear that she was Pete's mother, and not a romantic connection, but…

*   *   *

"Lois, it's John." Her hesitation told him she feared he was calling about something wrong, and he hurried to set her mind at ease. "Everything's fine here. I just heard something that might interest you." He filled her in on the details of his meeting with Larry, and their need for a transcriber. He described the work-at-home arrangements outlined by Larry, and gave her Larry's two numbers.

"Would I be living at your ranch?" She seemed incredulous.

"Yes. That way you could see Pete all the time and still have a job — and live in the countryside you were emoting over a while ago."

"I'll call him right away. Thank you, John."

Twenty minutes later his phone rang. "John! We've agreed! He's sending me the paperwork to do, and get in the return mail. I'll give my resignation here next Monday, and will start the first of next month. Oh! How will I get everything packed and ready to go by then? It's all so sudden!"

"Well, first, calm down. Pete and I will fly down there and get everything loaded and ready to go, so when moving day comes along all you'll have to do is say the word and it'll all be on the way."

"Oh, and John — I'll be making half again what I'm getting here!" The excitement in her voice was making her speech sound fluttery, but John could understand. It must have been mighty lonely for her there by herself!

She continued going over the details that she wouldn't need to face for a week or two, but she just wanted to talk, and John liked hearing the sound of her voice, particularly as bubbling happy as she sounded now.

Suddenly her voice turned serious. "I'll have to sell the house! It hadn't dawned on me until just this minute. "I can't do all that's required in time. What'll I do?"

"Give Ralph a call. I'll bet he'll have an idea or two — and would probably be happy to take care of the deal for you."

"I hadn't thought of that. That's a good idea. But I'll miss them. I hadn't thought of that either!"

"We'll see them from time to time. Remember, the Cessna covers a lot of ground in a hurry."

"I couldn't impose on you like that!"

"Quit talking nonsense! I like the old geezer too. And Evelyn sets a scrumptious table, to boot."

Pete walked in from school just as John hung up the phone. John turned, pulled a scowling face, and said, "Looks like work on the Rebel will be set back awhile."

"How come?" Pete sounded indignant.

"We'll be busy getting your mother packed and ready to move out here." At Pete's incredulous look John laughed and told him of the developments.

Pete jumped up and slapped the ceiling beam, letting out a war-whoop, and then grabbed John in a bear-hug, dancing around and around. "Mom's coming to live with us! Waaa-Hooo!"

"YEEESSS!"

The two high-fived like a couple of overgrown kids.

*   *   *

The flight to Vancouver was one of dodging clouds and making a southerly end-run to escape some heavy weather, but all-in-all it wasn't bad. Lois was waiting at the airport to pick them up, and again they went to Ralph and Evelyn's. As could be expected, Evelyn had the table set and dinner ready to be brought in. After the amenities were concluded Ralph said, "I hear you're going to take our Lois away from us. That's good, her being close to Pete, but we'll miss her."

"Kamloops isn't all that far, and airplanes get there and back pretty fast. I imagine you'll want to see the ranch from time to time, and we have plenty of room to put you up when you visit. I might even put you to work now and again." John's grin confirmed his pleasure at the idea.

Time flew by with the required preparations. True to John's guess, Ralph was more than happy to handle the sale of Lois's house. He had made some calls around and decided to buy it himself for a rental property. They had two others, and a third, being close enough for them to easily keep an eye on it, would be a good investment. The appraiser would be out the next day to give them a price for them to work from. Lois was relieved that the house would stay in the family; it held memories.

The truck was loaded and the doors shut and sealed. All Lois had to take was her small suitcase and make-up case, and those would fit in the Cessna.

The doorbell rang and John answered it, as he was closest. Two scruffy youths stood, sloppy baggy pants heavy with grime, their jaws hanging slack. The larger of the two said, "We wanta see Pete."

"May I tell him who wants to see him?" John inquired.

"None o' yer business," the speaker replied, belligerently.

"You the Shugard boys?"

"What's it to ya?"

"Just curious." As John turned to call to Pete, he stepped out onto the porch. The look on his face said that he would rather not have seen these two, but here they were.

"What ya want?" His voice had gone back to the slovenly slurring speech.

"Wanna talk to ya. C'mon." The head nodded in a command to come outside.

"I'm busy. We don't have anything to talk about."

"The hell we don't! You owe us!" Somehow their dim minds had forgotten it was Pete who had been caught, not them.

"I don't owe you ANYTHING!" His voice had lost the slurring, and regained the crisp, assured tone he had grown into. "We don't live in the same world anymore. Go back to your gutter!"

Pete started to turn away, indicating the conversation was ended. The larger Shugard boy made a lunge to grab Pete's arm, and from nowhere John's fist did the same thing Pete remembered from almost a year ago in the ranch house kitchen. The THUNK it made set the Shugard lad to coughing up his lunch as he sprawled on the porch steps.

John turned to the other Shugard boy, "Take your brother and get lost. Pete doesn't live here anymore, and the new owner can get pretty mean, I hear. Hit the road and don't come back."

As he closed the door and turned, Ralph, who had been helping with the finishing touches, said, "Where'd you hear that I was mean?"

"I don't know whether you are or not. When riled, that is. Anyhow, they don't know you from Adam, and that thought might make them reluctant to come back and take out their spleen on the empty house. Their kind think like that. They also don't want to get hurt, and having had a taste of that, they'll go looking for easier fish to terrorize."

Ralph laughed and noted that the sample had been sufficient to get them promptly on their way without a backward glance.

Pete looked baffled and said, "I could have handled them, John. You didn't need to do that."

"I know you could, but you didn't have to get your hands dirty, since I had a strong urge to do just that. I've had it for some time, and now it's off my chest."

Pete still didn't fully understand, but shrugged, grinned at Ralph and John, and went back to collecting the bags and putting them in Ralph's car.

*   *   *

Life at the ranch settled into a pattern, with Lois's office set up in Uncle Gil's den on the first floor. John had debated as to what to do with that inviting room, with a large stone fireplace, Indian-design blankets on the walls and a window that looked north and west to the ridge, across a mile of grazing land. The only break in the view of nature was the group of radio towers at the repeater station on the ridge.

The few furniture pieces Lois had selected to bring were placed in her bedroom and the office. The computer was set up in a new "work-center," complete with printer and a UPS, an emergency power supply, and she was already swamped with work. The transcribing had been done for the past few weeks by Larry's wife, who was barely knowledgeable enough to handle about half of it. She'd been a nurse and was familiar with computers, but to be a transcriber takes a lot more than that. Lois had a lot to catch up with, and Larry was more than happy to pay overtime to get the backlog cleaned up.

John came silently into the room; she had, at his urging, had the room floored in a deep pile carpet, and the silent part of his entrance wasn't hard to accomplish. He stood well behind her as her fingers flew over the keys. Her ears were covered by the padded earphones of the audio unit, and she listened to the droning voice of Dr. Bertram Cohen talk his way through an aneurysm repair.

John was tired from the day's labors, but happy to have her cheerful presence around the house. There was a bunch of realistic-looking artificial flowers in a vase on her desk and the drapes were opened to look out across the expanse of the ranch. The curtains she had made during her vacation gave the room a cheery look. The scene gave him a sense of peace and tranquility he hadn't felt since he was a boy living with his parents.

He stood, enjoying the scene for several minutes, and then strode around beside her work-center and sat down in the chair there. She glanced up at him in surprise and flashed him a smile, continuing with her transcribing.

"I rented a movie for tonight," John said as she took a short breather. "Thought it would be good to get you away from this 'infernal machine' for the evening."

"Oh? What did you rent?"

He told her, and she nodded her approval. A few more minutes of flying fingers and she stopped again, keyed the message to the modem, and took off the head-phones, pushing the recorder button.

"What's the occasion?" she asked, leaning back and stretching. She took the cassette out of the recorder and tossed it onto the desk.

"None in particular. I just thought it was time you took a break, and tonight's a good time for it. Heard this movie is good for a few belly-laughs, and thought all of us hard-working stiffs could stand a night away from the grinding wheel. Where's Pete?"

"Went with Bob to see somebody's new car. New to him, that is."

She gazed out across the range and the mountain.

"Look at the shape of that part of the mountain — right above where we were stuck on the road. That slope ought to be great for skiing when it has snow on it. I remember thinking last winter when I was here that it should be a good slope. Do you ever ski?"

He shook his head sadly, "No. I've never had a pair on. I've never been into sports to any degree. Are you a skier?"

"Yes. I used to ski a lot before I was married, and Allan was sort of lukewarm about it. We went to Whistler a few times a year. That slope looks like it was made for a couple of interesting runs. Does it get a good snow cover every winter?"

"Yes. The prevailing wind in winter brings the clouds over the ridge and they dump a lot on this side as they go over. I guess they would make a good run — or two."

"Well, now that I'll be living here this winter, I just might try out this slope and see if we don't have our own ski-run. What do you think of that!" Her perky grin set John to laughing. She was an engaging woman. "I might even teach you to ski. Peter had a good start when Allan was killed, and after that we couldn't afford it."

*   *   *

Work on the Rebel had stalled while they moved Lois to the ranch, and now, with winter just over the horizon, the winter preparations kept them too tired to spend their evenings in the shop. The cattle would winter on the ranch fields; the altitude here didn't make for too harsh conditions for them, and there were several large groves of trees — evergreens — that would provide adequate shelter for the small herd John had. Of course, feed would have to be hauled out to the animals, but that wasn't at all unusual in these latitudes. That was when progress on the Rebel should be made.

It was mid-September when a letter to Lois was received from the court in Vancouver. It directed her to appear before a magistrate on October 7th and bring her son, Peter. There was also a letter addressed to John, containing a court order for him to appear at the same date and time.

The next couple weeks were filled with a sense of foreboding. What could be the trouble? Pete certainly hadn't been in any trouble since he'd been here, and all the previous problems had been taken care of.

This trip they had to drive; the weather was a cold drizzle, which promised to break into a serious rainstorm. Of course the drive was about four hours in good weather, and in rain, maybe 5. The road was good all the way and snow wasn't predicted.

They took Uncle Gil's Chrysler station wagon, and stayed with Ralph and Evelyn. Their house was big enough, and no hotels were needed. It also made a good excuse to visit the grandparents. The trip was, however, subdued because of the unknown nature of the summons.

On the 7th the three entered the court, reported to the clerk, and took seats as directed. The usual hum-drum of court procedure continued, until the magistrate entered. There was the usual standing and then seating, and the magistrate shuffled papers for about ten minutes, conferring from time to time with the clerk in hushed voices.

"We'll deal with the case of Mr. Peter Milner first. Will he come forward to the bar, along with his mother and Mr. John Morgan."

They rose and went forward, John and Lois standing on both sides of Pete.

"Mr. Morgan, I have here several papers pertaining to young Mr. Milner, here; reports, I believe, to Mr. Quincy Ellersbee, Probation Officer in Mr. Milner's case. Did you in fact write these letters?"

"I wrote letters, Sir. I can't say if those are the ones, but I wrote one each week that Pete was with me."

"That's good enough. I also have here letters from Mr. Ellersbee, and reports, along with his recommendation that, in view of Mr. Milner's conduct since his probation, and in view of the fact that he is no longer in contact with certain persons, and is presently gainfully employed while attending school regularly, that his probation be revoked and terminated. There also is a report from a Captain William Forger of the Royal Canadian Mounted Police describing Mr. Milner's actions while assisting in the rescue of passengers from a crashed Wescan Airlines airplane.

"There seems no longer any reason to keep you on the books, Mr. Milner. You are therefore free of any and all restrictions and constraints of this court, and all charges against you in the past are to be expunged. Congratulations, Mr. Milner. And you are a lucky young man to have a friend like Mr. Morgan. That is all. You are free to go."

A stunned and happy trio walked out of the courtroom. It was only 9:30 and none of them had been interested in breakfast before the court hearing. Now they were. As they sat down at the restaurant table Lois said, "I think a short prayer of thanks is in order."

Chapter 8
A Three-Way Bear-Hug

The storm turned to snow about halfway to Kamloops, and John and Pete turned-to and put the chains on. The steady pock-a-pock of the wind-shield wiper was lulling John to sleep, and Lois noticed him blinking and shaking his head to clear it.

"Why don't I drive for awhile?" she said.

At John's surprised look she replied, "I've driven many a mile in snow. Anyone raised in Canada has to." It was her way of easing the hint that John was getting dangerously drowsy, he now realized.

She had been driving for about an hour when the car a couple of hundred yards ahead of them began weaving erratically. Lois backed off another hundred yards, and in about another mile or so the other car veered into the oncoming lane, fortunately empty, and then, over-correcting, slewed onto the shoulder. The front wheel struck the edge berm and the 4-door sedan rolled over, across the top, and came to rest on its right side.

Lois braked, pulling over and putting on her hazard lights.

John had been dozing, but now was wide awake at Lois's call when the other car began weaving. Stepping out as soon as the wagon stopped, he ran to the wreck. The driver had been thrown clear before the car overturned and was lying on the roadway, unconscious. John quickly checked him for signs of bleeding and found he wasn't breathing.

"Pete, quick! Give me a hand."

Quickly loosening the man's collar he began Cardio-Pulmonary Resuscitation, CPR. Pete joined him, giving regular chest thrusts while John tilted the man's head back to open his airway, pinched his nose closed and gave him mouth-to-mouth resuscitation. Within about five minutes the victim coughed, gasped, and was breathing on his own, and his pulse was also OK.

Lois had also been busy. The highway wasn't deserted and she had called in the emergency on the Channel 9 emergency frequency and was directing traffic, having enlisted others to caution oncoming traffic while they had the distance to stop.

There was handshaking and backslapping, and the inevitable police report to fill out. The Highway Patrolman made note of the medics' comments that the almost immediate provision of CPR had certainly saved the man's life, that there might be internal injuries, but that the man would probably survive because of their actions.

This was the first time Lois had seen her son in action in an emergency. The trip home was filled with conversation.

"How did you come to know CPR, Pete?" she asked.

"The Barriere Fire Department offered a night-school course in it and we both took it. Knowing stuff like that's a necessity, working on a ranch as isolated as we are, so we went. It came in handy today."

Lois noted that it was Pete that spoke up, and he did it so off-handedly that she was once more reminded of how he'd matured since coming under John's influence. His evaluation of Pete as a responsible young man now seemed fully justified.

*   *   *

Winter had settled in, and snow had been falling for a week. The shop was cozy with the wood-burning heater and insulation, and real progress was being made with the Rebel. The tail-feathers had been completed and the fuselage was beginning to look like a good part of an airplane. John was thinking he'd better start looking for an engine, as there were several fuselage components that had to be configured for whatever engine was to be installed.

Each morning, feed had to be hauled out to the tree clumps providing shelter for the herd, and the water trough was checked to make sure it wasn't iced-over. Lois had breakfast ready for them when they came in, snow-covered and cold, shedding parkas, gloves and hats. Then it was time for the "boys" to go into the shop and get to work, and Lois to set up her audio and computer for transcribing.

She had pretty well caught up with the backlog and was finding time to take breaks to help with the plane. She had quickly become expert at pulling rivets with the pliers-like rivet puller, and some-times John and Pete, fitting parts, were hard-pressed to stay ahead of her. Fortunately, in this kit, the rivet holes were pre-punched in the aluminum, and drilling was held to a minimum. "Cleco" clamps in rivet holes held parts together while being riveted.

The extension phone in the shop rang and Lois answered it.

"Is John Morgan there?" The voice was deep and scratchy.

"Yes he is. Right here." She handed the handset to John.

"John Morgan here."

There was a pause of a few seconds, then, "Well, hello Dad! You're sure sounding good. Your ticker doing better?"

There was a long pause while he listened, then he spoke again: "Yes. I can come up there for a few days. This weather is supposed to let up by the weekend, and I can rent a plane and fly up. Yes, I'd like to very much. I'll see you then, even if I have to drive. Bye."

Turning to the others, a thoughtful look on his face, he said, "That was my dad. Last time I spoke with him, well over a month ago, he sounded very down. Like he was waiting to die. It was very depressing. Now he's asking me to come up to Calgary to meet his new lady-friend! He sounds like a new man."

"How old is he?" Lois asked.

"Sixty six, I think. When Mom died he said life wasn't worth living without her. At first I thought it was just the immediate grief, but he sold the business and retired. Soon he was just sitting around, waiting to die. I don't understand it! What's made the change?"

Lois smiled but said nothing. Pete said, "You going up there this week-end?"

"Yes. He sounded so anxious to have me meet this woman that I couldn't refuse. It's about 400 miles, and if the roads are clear I usually make it in seven and a half hours. If the weather's good, I can fly it in about five hours if I refuel at Golden."

"That's an awfully long drive by yourself, John. If the weather doesn't clear by the week-end, we could go with you and I can help with the driving. And, Peter and I can see Calgary while you visit with your father and his friend. That way we can trade off the driving and you'll be more rested when you get there."

This left John with a dilemma. This new "lady-friend" could turn out to be just after his money — of which there wasn't all that great an amount — or after the house, which was large and still worth quite a bit. What's she after?

"Yes, I guess so. But it may be embarrassing. I don't know who this 'lady-friend' is, and she may be someone trying to take advantage of a lonely old man. So, things may get unpleasant. If it does, I beg your pardon in advance. And I thank you for the help."

John prayed fervently for good flying weather, but it snowed.

They left Friday morning, taking the 4-wheel drive Land Cruiser, and made the trip in ten hours. Although it snowed the entire journey, the temperature was relatively mild.

With the weather as it was John had called his dad before they left and asked if he had room for them all. He and Pete could occupy one room, and Lois another. With no more information than he had, it had occurred to him that the 'lady-friend' might be in residence, and he didn't want to have to find a motel late at night.

There was room for them all, and on arrival they all trooped into the house amid snowflakes. Glenn greeted them, and John's appraisal of his father's condition made him do a double-take. He was standing straight and his eye had the old "hawk-look" from under bushy eyebrows. His handshake was firm, and John was glad to see his father in such good health, even if the cause for it might be — almost certainly was — just after what there was of his money, or the house. His suspicions were dying hard.

Glenn turned and called up the stairs, "Janet, they're here."

The tall lady descending the stairs a minute later looked more familiar to John with each blink.

"Janet Monroe? Well, this is a surprise!"

Turning to Lois and Pete he introduced them and explained, "Janet and Hal had been Dad and Mother's closest friends many years ago, when Garry and I were growing up. Our two families took trips together and attended the same church, and often either went to dinner together or were at one house or the other. Alex, their son, was one of my closest friends through high school, and we still correspond occasionally. Alex wrote me of his father's death some years back, but by then the Monroes had moved to the States."

Janet smiled graciously as John told this, and added, "I've just recently moved back to our old house. You remember my sister,

Louise? She passed away last year, and the house has been vacant since. I had nothing tying me to Seattle any longer, and decided I'd come back and live here in Calgary, where all my old friends are. And how are you doing as a cattle rancher, John?"

The conversation went on as they moved their bags into the house and Janet told them that she'd prepared a hot meal for them, as she figured they'd be frozen after the long trip. John gave her a brief run-down on Pete and Lois and the current situation, stressing the help he'd received from Pete. He left out reference to Pete's legal troubles, and left it that Pete was disenchanted with city life, which was true enough.

During the dinner, late though it was, Lois hit it off well with Janet while Pete and Glenn were becoming buddies. Later they relaxed in the living room and John, Glenn and Janet talked over old times, explaining as they went to Lois and Pete. Before the evening was over they were all comfortable together, and it was with reluctance that they broke it up and went their separate ways to slumberland.

It devolved that Janet had moved back to her old house and she and Glenn had met in the supermarket a few days later. She didn't know that he had been widowed, nor did he know she had moved back to Calgary, and both were surprised. A lunch together at a local restaurant carried over to a dinner at her house, and she challenged him to a round of golf the following morning. From those beginnings it became an everyday event, going to shows and the museum and the park. Winter had then been just around the corner and they'd made the most of the good weather.

"The latest development, Son, is that next Wednesday we are going to be married!"

"What?!" John almost came out of his chair.

"What's the matter? Don't you think I've known the lady long enough?"

110

"But I — I guess — but you're almost — well — like family." The truth that they were two mature single adults finally soaked in and a big, wide grin broke out. "I think it's wonderful!" he gasped at last.

He strode over, wrapped Janet in a bear-hug and planted a big kiss on her cheek, "Just like the old days when I'd kiss Auntie Janet! But you won't be 'Auntie' any more."

His happy excitement was contagious. The women began talking about wedding things and John and his dad began talking about them coming out and visiting the ranch.

* * *

The weekend stretched to Thursday. After the wedding Glenn and Janet took a plane for Seattle to honeymoon, and then visit her sister there, leaving the other three to close up the house when they left for Kamloops and the ranch. The rest of Wednesday John took Lois and Pete on a tour of the city and his old haunts, but most of his old friends were gone, and the day was spent enjoying themselves. Thursday was a long day of driving, but the weather cooperated and the sun was bright and warm, getting rid of the remaining snow on the roads.

On Tuesday Glenn and John had gone on a few errands together and ended up at a restaurant for lunch. John had confessed to his dad about his misgivings about the "new lady-friend," and the relief when he found out it was Janet.

"How did it happen?" he asked as they were seated.

"Very simple, John. I was lonely. You might say I was dying of loneliness. When you've been married to a good woman for a lifetime, and she passes away, it's like dying yourself. That's how I felt. Some other woman wouldn't do. It had to be someone of her quality, and Janet fills that bill. She'll never replace your mother — no one ever could. But she will give me a few more happy years. As for money, Hal left her better off than I am.

"I've never been disloyal to your mother, but there were many times back then that I wondered what kind of wife Janet would be. Not fantasizing, but just admiring a fine woman. Now, I guess, I'm going to find out. Not that I wished it that way — God knows I'd have your mother back in a moment if I could, but I can't. So, life goes on, and it's sure looking up for me."

"I understand, Dad, and I was worried about you; you seemed to be going downhill fast."

"Janet took care of that! She just wouldn't let me sit an' die like I was doing. She got me interested in living again. It's wonderful what love can do for a man."

"If you say so, Dad. My experience hasn't been so good in that department, though."

"What's with you and this Lois? She looks like a fine woman. Isn't it about time you got over that dingbat Dorie?"

"Dad, I just can't tie myself down with a wife right now! I've got the ranch, but the cattle business is down. Some luck saved my hide this year, but what about next year? What would I do with a wife when I can't even figure how I'm going to support myself?"

"Did you ever think that a wife might help you figure it out?"

"It wouldn't be fair to her."

"Lord sakes, Kid. Wake up. You're past thirty six now, 'nother couple years you'll be forty. That woman looks at you like she thinks you're God. And I'm a judge of good women."

"Don't push, Dad."

* * *

The weather was the kind that allowed just the bare minimum of outdoor work, and progress on the Rebel was being made. The newest issue of Sport Aviation arrived, and the ad for a Lycoming O-

235-C jumped right out of the page at John. With a matching propeller, too, and the price was right. The phone got a workout, followed by a visit to the bank, which produced a certified check; the latter was on its way the next afternoon. It took three weeks for the crated Lyc to arrive, and it was late that night before John and Pete knocked off and turned in.

John was on cloud nine. The engine was in beautiful shape and the logs were up-to-date. It had only 18 hours on it since major overhaul to factory tolerances, and the propeller was just as good.

John had a friend in Kamloops who was a certified welder and the two of them fabricated an engine mount a few days later. The fuselage was taking shape and by next week would be "on the gear", meaning the landing gear would be supporting the airplane. That's a milestone for any aircraft builder.

John's conversation with his dad in the restaurant kept coming back to haunt him. Yes, she is a fine woman! Forget Dorie. But that's not all. It wouldn't be fair to saddle Lois with me — when I still can't figure what to do to make a living. I sure can't live off her income! And the ranch won't cut it, not with the pitiful herd I have. Even with a bigger herd, with beef prices where they were, it wouldn't be enough.

* * *

Among the things Lois had brought were her skis, and the recent snows had made her anxious to try them out. A week after their return she talked John into taking her up to the ridge on the horses, and she'd try the slope while he brought the horses back down. He was somewhat dubious, but she prevailed, and by the time he was at the bottom he met a glowing and bubbly Lois, who reported a first rate run.

"It's a good slope. Not Whistler, but fun." All the way back to the house she enthused.

Days passed with the routine of hauling feed and working on the Rebel. The excitement of building the plane had come down to a daily routine, and was becoming almost a grind. The weather had precluded any flying for two months.

Ted Waddell called and asked for John. Ted was a neighboring rancher who also used his airplane for commuting to various cities and other ranches on business, and John had flown his 172 a time or two in the past.

"John, I have a proposition for you. The drive into Kamloops takes a lot of time when I need to fly somewhere on business — or pleasure. Out behind your barn is a nice flat spot with plenty of clear, flat ground to make a nice airstrip. You're building your Rebel, and will soon want to be test-flying it, and presumably would rather fly it from a local field than have to haul it clear in to Kamloops."

"I think I get your drift. Quit beatin' around the bush, Ted," John said. The same idea had been tickling his mind lately. He was all ears.

Ted continued, "I just bought a dismantled metal building that will be just the ticket for a modest hangar. I was talking with Jack Perkins — you know, the gent with the Maule — and he has connections to get some paving done for cheap. And, my back lot has too much slope to it for any kind of strip.

"Here's what I propose: if you'll provide the land and do the earthwork with your 'dozer, I'll throw in the building and erect it on foundations you build. After you have the strip and a ramp dozed and ready, Jack will pave the strip and ramp. That way all three of us will have a strip right here in our own backyard, and won't have to spend two hours to get to Kamloops and back every time we want to fly."

"Sounds good. How'll we work the legal angle? Form a company?"

"Makes sense. If we put it all down on paper, we avoid misunderstandings later. Think on it, and get back to me."

"Ted, I've already done the thinking. Let's do it. My lawyer is Jerry Wilson in Kamloops. I'll call him and have him put together an agreement, and then you, Jack and I can get together and iron out anything we need to, and get the show on the road. I've had the idea in the back of my mind for some time, and I think the time has come. I also have a topo map of the ranch my uncle had made years ago, and I can make a layout of the strip, drainage and a ramp and foundations so we can go ahead as soon as the weather permits. Also, I have a better location for it than behind my barn — alongside the highway, about 500 yards your side of the house. It's flatter and with better take-off and landing approaches. How does that grab ya?"

* * *

The work on the Rebel had started with the empennage, and that had been completed and hung in the rafters to be out of the way and protected from "hangar rash." John had chosen to build the wing next and hang it overhead while building the fuselage.

The fuselage would take up a lot of floor space in the shop while building. The fuselage was now "on the gear" and the engine hung in the mounts on her nose. Of course, without the weight of the empennage and the wings aft of the gear, she would tend to nose over — which would be disastrous to the engine, so a sack of sand was laid across the fuselage just ahead of the tail to hold it down.

* * *

Christmas was one such as John had not seen in a long time. They had a tree; Lois had brought decorations among her treasures when she moved here, and the house was looking like a family lived in it. Shopping trips into Kamloops had packages under the tree and goodies on the table. While he'd been living here by himself, such holidays had been quite Spartan, since there had been no one to share them with, and last Christmas he and Pete had driven to Vancouver to spend it with Lois, Ralph and Evelyn.

But this was different. He was in his own home and had a family — of sorts — around him. This was the first time since he'd been home, before he'd gone off to college, that he'd had this kind of holiday celebration. The one while he was married to Dorie had been just a dinner at the country club with acquaintances of hers — and too much booze.

He wasn't a tee-totaler, but the way her crowd drank, it wasn't relaxing and friendly; it was more like a competition. Everyone seemed to be trying to outdo everyone else at being smart, catty and cutting with their comments, which left John feeling that he was in the wrong company. Friends were for relaxation and enjoyment; with Dorie's crowd it was a dogfight by the end of the evening, and the headache and sour stomach on Christmas morning wasn't his idea of a pleasant day. So much for Dorie's way of life!

There was two feet of snow on the ground Christmas morning. After opening presents all around, they went outside and played in the fresh, powdery snow, throwing snowballs and washing each other's faces with snow. John had a huge handful of snow and caught Lois unawares, pushing the wad of snow squarely into her laughing face. She tried dodging him and fell, pulling him down with her.

She lay in the snow, laughing, with John lying half on top of her, and without conscious thought, he pulled her to him and kissed her ardently. Her laugh was so infectious that he had been laughing too, and suddenly they were both silent. She had returned his kiss just as ardently, and they lay in the snow, looking wonderingly into each others' eyes.

He helped her stand, and she held onto his hand, saying gently, "I guess that was inevitable, John. Did you mean it as much as I did?"

"I guess I did — do. I guess it's been in my mind for a long time." He bent and kissed her again, this time gently and tenderly. Yes, I guess it's about time I forgot Dorie! Lois is an entirely different kind of woman. The only way I can be any happier than I am now is to marry her. Dad's not so dumb after all!

He found himself facing her, looking solemnly into her eyes, and hers were returning the look. "Lois, would you do me the honor of marrying me?" It was simple and straightforward.

Her answer was just as straightforward, "Yes, John. I've been wanting to hear that question for some time now. When do you want to be married?"

"Yesterday! But seriously, when would it be best for you?"

"I'd like yesterday, too, but from a practical standpoint, next week — say Wednesday — would be more realistic. I'd like to have Ralph and Evelyn here, and can we be married in this house? I've come to love it as though I'd lived here all my life."

Pete had been watching all this with mixed emotions, and when he learned they were to be married, he rushed over and hugged his mother. Turning to John, he said, "And you're going to be my dad!"

"Seems like I've spent about a year being just about that. I'm proud to call you Son."

There was a three-way bear-hug as Ted and Julie drove up to share some Christmas cheer and talk about the airstrip. Ted's present to John was a bright orange wind-sock.

*   *   *

The wedding was small and quiet, with only Pete, Ralph and Evelyn, and some of John's neighbors and friends — like Evan, Joan and Bob Keenawah, Ted and Julie, and Jack and Ruth. And Glenn and Janet. As the ceremonies ended, John turned to the elder Morgan and said, "Looks like you were right, Dad."

The week's honeymoon to Seattle was quiet and private and the weather cooperated. Ralph and Evelyn stayed with Pete. John and

Lois spent a beautiful week enjoying the out-of-the-way places Seattle can provide. They rented a Cessna 152, taking an air-tour of the San Juan Islands and inlets and out over the rain forest of the Olympic Peninsula. And they spent long hours relaxing and talking of their likes and dislikes and hopes and worries, dreams and wishes.

*   *   *

John had his drafting table set up in the office, now sharing occupancy of what had been Lois' office. The information from the old topo map was transferred to the drawing of the airstrip taking shape. The optimum place for the airstrip wasn't behind the barn, but near the road and a little less than half a mile north of the house. This would permit a separate driveway from the road, and allow the others to have access without disturbing the family. The ramp and hangar would be located about the middle of the 4,300 foot strip; power could be brought in from the lines along the road that served their ranches without too much trouble, obviating the need for either long, expensive lines or a generator. Electrical conduits were placed across under the runway for future lighting.

Drawings for the hangar foundations were furnished with the building, the components of which were now stored adjacent to the hangar site, ready for erection when the weather permitted. The prevailing wind was almost parallel to the road, allowing better layout of the strip, hangar and ramp.

Chapter 9
A New Name for Morgan Ranch

Routine around the house continued about the same as before, except of course Lois had relocated her sleeping arrangements, and the master bedroom had taken on the appearance of having a woman in residence. Clothes were rearranged in the closets; at first John wasn't sure he liked the new orderliness, but the more he lived with it the more comfortable he became with it.

Another facet that he hadn't thought about before the wedding was that of being welcomed into the arms of this woman without the smell of booze and cigarettes on her breath, and the distraction of contentiousness. That was only one of the grating things that marred his past experience with married life. How different Lois is from Dorie! There was a mutual affection shown throughout their days, and their nights were blessed with warmth and caring.

This is what I always thought marriage was like, John mused — the little familiar things like a kiss when passing in the hallway, the smile and wink at shared thoughts at the table, the touch of her hand on his face as sleep overtook them.

* * *

Time passed and work progressed on the Rebel; the wing was taking shape and the wet-cell fuel tanks were being prepared before closing the last sheets of skin and riveting them in place. By now all three of them considered themselves "airplane builders." The local chapter of EAA had held a meeting at their shop, and many had come to help, or just watch and give advice, much of which was valid. Several of them had been this route themselves, and were very knowledgeable about airplanes.

Each stage of construction was inspected by the DOT inspector, after the EAA chapter's Technical Councilor had looked it over. The shop bookshelves were loaded with EAA technical publications, and the walls with photos, plans and completed components not yet ready for installation.

Pete wore his EAA jacket and hat to school with obvious pride, while the shop had long since become a hangout for Pete's school friends on afternoons and weekends. There were often several willing hands to hold this, bring the box of rivets, or whatever.

And Shirley.

She now had a driver's license, and borrowed her dad's pickup on weekends to join the aircraft's crew. Pete had also received his driver's license recently, which meant he could run errands into town for them. John had finally bought a used refrigerator for the "shop" and stocked it with soft drinks and candy bars — all this free labor was worth something.

Many of those helping hands had viewed the several videos of Oshkosh Fly-Ins and other regional ones. Afternoons, after school and while the snow precluded field work, there were always at least two or three hanging around the shop and the sound of roaring engines and revving propellers could be heard in their conversation, commonly known as "hangar flying".

* * *

The snows were fast disappearing and the Rebel now had her wing mounted. She was still inside the shop, and they would have to take the wing back off to get her out, but it allowed fit-up of all the fuel lines, wiring for lights, fuel gauges and radio antenna. She was a beauty. They had decided that since they had been extra-careful handling the aluminum skins, and they were unscratched and shiny, the airplane would be left unpainted. Paint adds weight, and any weight saved was available for additional baggage or better performance. There was one unsightly scratch in the vertical fin, but it could be easily incorporated into the decorative trim of red and blue. Several times Lois or John had gone to the shop to see Pete sitting in the left seat, pretending to be flying her. There's still some boy left in that young man, John thought, but I guess there's still quite a bit of it in me, too. Any man, I guess.

John estimated the date for test-flight would be some time in late June. The engine had been run, and all systems worked — in the shop. What a sweet sound that Lycoming put out!

During the Spring, John had started Pete in flight school with Jerry, and, with Pete able to put in two to four hours in the air each weekend that the weather was decent, he soon took the DOT inspector for a ride, and came home with his temporary Private Pilot's License. He was now certified to fly his mother wherever she wanted to go, and he did take her for a couple of hours of sightseeing. Or to take a Cessna out and cruise over the mountain ridges and forests by himself. The next weekend he took Shirley for a ride, and she, too, was hooked. Bob and he went for several local flights; Bob paid for the gas and Pete the "dry" rental.

* * *

Ralph had called one evening and asked if someone was going to be home Thursday. John had said yes, and asked why, and Ralph had said that a friend was coming up that way and would drop something off. Thursday rolled around and at mid-morning a large commercial van pulled into the ranch yard. The driver and another man, both wearing overalls, rang the bell and asked Lois where the shop was, and she directed them there. John was working on the Rebel, and as the truck backed to the door he became aware of its presence.

The driver asked, "You John Morgan?"

"Yes."

"Well, we've got some machinery to deliver to you. Here's a note from the sender."

He handed John an envelope, and after lifting a pair of large cardboard boxes out of the way, began dragging out several large heavy crates and setting them inside the shop. The envelope went into John's pocket and a 2-wheel handcart was produced to help.

"Are you sure this is the right place?" John asked the driver.

He looked at his clip board and replied, "Yup! You're John Morgan, ain't ya? And this is the right address?"

John looked at the address on the manifest and agreed.

"Then it's for you!"

One crate was about six feet long by about two feet square, and there were small square boxes and some large ones, some were cardboard and some wood. They were all heavy.

After the last was unloaded the driver held the clipboard out for John to sign. It said simply, "Fourteen boxes of machinery parts." John counted, agreed with the number, and signed.

As the van drove off, a prybar was produced and the opening began. The long, skinny one contained the bed of an old South Bend lathe, likely built in the late 1920's. Next there was a tailstock, and as the boxes gave up their goods, all the components of a metal lathe and a bench milling machine emerged. Smaller boxes held a Kennedy tool chest filled with micrometers, dial gauges, parallels, all types of measuring instruments and many lathe cutting tools. Another box held dozens of assorted milling cutters.

Suddenly John remembered the envelope and took it from his pocket, smoothing out the wrinkles. He opened the envelope and read;

> John,
>
> These tools belonged to my brother. They've been taking up room in storage and costing me money, and were getting lonesome for someone who could put them to work.
>
> Ralph

As John was wiping away the moisture that filled his eyes, Lois arrived to see what was going on, and stood aghast at the machinery. He silently handed the note to her. She read it twice, just to make sure.

"Oh, John! Wasn't that nice of him!"

There was a phone in the shop but he didn't have Ralph's number out here, and went into the house to call.

That night John sat in their shared office and his thoughts strayed to the decision he and Lois had to make. Lois was diligently turning speech from the recording tape to words on her computer screen. She reached the end of the tape and shut it off, adding some coding to the computer readout. She transmitted it by modem to the hospital records machine and recorded it on her file diskette, storing it in her file box.

John's gesture interrupted her reach for another audio tape. Lois dropped the new audio tape into the player and turned to look out the large window at the mountain. John joined her and they silently gazed at the majesty of the ridge. Similar thoughts had been running through both their minds: Just what are we going to do with the ranch now?

*　*　*

As soon as the local snow had melted and the Cat could get on the ground without bogging down, John had the airstrip bladed and Jack's surveyor was giving him signals for the final leveling cuts. A good heavy rain washed some soil into it, but a day's work repaired that, and a string of Jack's trucks hauling crusher-run aggregate — crushed hard rock — covered the area with 10 inches of base. Jack had to wait until the daily temperature was above 45°F. before he could pave with the asphalt, but the weatherman cooperated and by the end of a warm week, the paving was done.

Meanwhile John had borrowed Jack's backhoe and dug trenches for a sound foundation for the hangar. Pete and John finished the forms and rebar the following week, and the foundation walls were poured that weekend. The concrete floor was then poured for the hangar and the ramp. It was a busy Spring!

Ted's ironworkers made short work of erecting the prefab building. Originally designed as a standard 50 x 100 foot farm building, it would, with judicious placement, house three Cessna 172-sized airplanes, with plenty of room behind each for shop and office space for records and flight planning. The basic building had been modified to have one wide sliding door in each end, and one centered in the side facing the ramp.

The following weekend both Ted's 172 and Jack's Bonanza flew in to their new "home." In the fading light Ted, Jack, Pete, Lois and John stood on the ramp looking at the two planes. The Rebel would soon join them.

True to this, the following Monday the Rebel wing was removed, the bird was wheeled out of the shop, and the wing re-installed. Wiring and fuel lines were soon re-connected and all bolts torqued to specs. Fuel went into the tanks and John crawled into the cockpit, tried the foot-brakes for stiffness, turned the fuel valve to left tank, and pumped the primer.

He called "Clear", to warn anyone outside of the pilot's sight that an airplane was about to be started, and turned the switch. The propeller flipped over four turns as the starter whined and the plane shuddered, and then, with blue smoke belching out of the stacks, it started with a smooth roar. The Rebel was already eager. John taxied her to the hangar in the late glow of afternoon, and put her to bed in her new home. Again, the three stood, looking admiringly at their bird in the hangar.

"Going to test her tomorrow, John?" Pete asked over the venison pot roast that night. Lois looked askance at John. She had seen old movies of the trauma of test flights, and was viewing this as something to be dreaded. She hadn't been present during the earlier months when Pete and John had read the EAA manuals, including the ones on recommended practices for testing. All airplanes are different, and what works best with one may not for another. But there were a set of procedures to follow to safely test any airplane, and although both the men understood what was to be done, neither realized that Lois was completely in the dark on all this.

So it was the next morning that Lois was having difficulty keeping from gnawing her fingernails, and as she heard the Lyc fire up, she came to the back door to watch. She was relieved and disappointed. All John did was taxi the airplane up and down the runway and taxiway.

Then he'd get out and make an adjustment somewhere, get back in, fire it up, and taxi some more. He grabbed a wing-tip and rocked the airplane. Then he let some air out of the tires, checked the pressures, and rocked the airplane. He got the portable air tank and put some air back into the tires, checked them again, and rocked the airplane again. Then he got back in and taxied back and forth some more. Bored, she returned to the house and her transcribing.

It was almost lunchtime when she heard the engine roaring and she ran to the porch again. John had the Rebel up on her main gear and tearing down the runway. Then the roar died and the plane slowed, turning off and taxiing back to the other end. Again he made a high speed run, stopping just before it would lift off, and then turned to do it again. This time it wobbled a bit as he walked the rudder pedals, and the next time it was the ailerons. Again Lois gave up in disgust and went indoors to fix lunch. When she waved from the porch, John parked the Rebel and came on in.

"Just what are you doing out there? I thought you were going to test the Rebel!"

"I am. The first thing in testing is to check out the ground handling and adjustments. Like, are the brakes too soft or too sharp? Either of those could put you into a ball of crumpled aluminum if you found out too late. And all this while you watch the gauges. With an untried airplane the oil may get too hot with just taxiing. That would indicate that you might not be getting enough air to the oil radiator. Air flows are squirrelly. Then if a cylinder head temperature gauge shows excessive heat, it might indicate that some baffling around the cylinders is inadequate or needs adjustment.

"Then, how effective is the rudder? On the runway, open her up a little and test the elevator response, the rudder response and the ailerons. Then, when you're completely familiar with what to expect from THIS airplane, you can take off, stay near the field where you can make it back if the engine quits, and land. Get the feel of the bird. Then go on to altitude and try out the stall characteristics and general handling characteristics, staying close enough to the field so you can make it back if anything quits or isn't right."

"But what if the engine quits? Won't you crash?"

"You've been up with me and Pete. Haven't you noticed that when we want to come down and land, we slow the engine down, and finally shut it down to just an idle?"

"Yes. But what's that got to do with it?"

"Lois! If the engine quits, and I have a place to land, I just glide in and land."

Her expression told him that the light had dawned.

"You see, it takes the engine to go up, and to stay in the air, but to come down you remove the power and the airplane glides as long as there's air beneath her wheels, and then, you put them on the pavement. You've seen too many old Clark Gable movies!"

When Pete arrived home from school he and John huddled for a few minutes about the testing thus far, and the actual flight this afternoon. John had Pete take a couple of taxi runs and then a high speed run, and when Pete got out he went to the left aileron where the little metal trim tab was located and gave it a small tweak.

"Felt a little heavy on the left. See if that doesn't feel better," he said as John came up. "Ready to test her upstairs, Dad?"

That was the first time he had used the pronoun, and John noticed, but said nothing. He grinned, nodded and climbed into the cockpit.

Lighting off the Lyc, he wheeled the bird onto the taxiway and, after a run-up and final trim check, poured on the coal. The tail was up almost instantly and within a hundred yards she was grabbing air. Like a balloon! John had to trim the nose up to keep her airspeed in the optimum 70 mph range, and he leveled off at pattern altitude before the logical point for turning onto crosswind departure had been reached — she was a climber!

Of course he only had himself, no baggage and half a tank of fuel, but she did considerably better than 1,000 feet per minute. Not at all shabby! Staying in a close pattern, he brought her around and made a slightly long final, trying out the glide characteristics and staying well above the published stall speed — just in case.

The three things most useless to a pilot are altitude above him, runway behind him and fuel already burned. To that may be added one more: airspeed you don't have!

Taxiing back to the head end of the runway, giving Pete and Lois the "four-oh" signal of thumb and forefinger forming an O as he passed them, he now took off and climbed to 6,000 feet and leveled off. With full power on he pulled the nose up further and further until the rate of climb indicator needle fell past the zero, and the controls became mushy and fluttery feeling. The final stall was mild and the nose simply fell through, the right wing dropping slightly. Correcting with rudder, he was able to hold the bird in a straight-forward mush, losing altitude, but not falling off significantly to either side. No vicious stall characteristics! Engine temperatures still normal — still getting adequate cooling in a stall.

Letting the stick forward to neutral, the nose quickly dropped and the airspeed came up rapidly. The controls resumed their normal slight stiffness in level flight.

Pulling on carburetor heat and closing the throttle, he again eased the stick back until the stall was reached, with no drastic results, either. Good! This airplane had no scary bad habits — in fact no bad habits that he'd been able to discern. Oil temperatures and pressures were staying in the green and her performance was well within the published parameters.

With the sun nearing the horizon and the fuel gauge showing ¼ he dropped the nose, entered the pattern, and landed.

There was jubilation in the ranch house that evening. After dinner John went to the shop refrigerator and brought in a bottle of champagne. "I've been saving this for tonight. I don't think it will hurt Pete, in his tender years, to share a toast to the Rebel. And I propose a toast to a new name for Morgan Ranch: Rebel Ranch!"

Pete seemed furtive the next few days, then, at breakfast one day he went out to the shop with a sneaky grin. He returned ten minutes later with a 4' x 4' piece of plywood covered by a large piece of brown paper of the sort many of the Rebel's parts had been covered with for shipment.

Placing the plywood on the floor to lean against a chair across the room from Lois and John, seated at the kitchen table, he turned to them, still with the silly grin on his face, and swept the paper away.

There, across the sky-blue painted board, a very accurate picture of the Rebel in flight was painted. In the upper left corner, in orange letters, was lettered REBEL, and in the lower right corner was RANCH.

* * *

Things went back to normal, but this summer John had Lois to ride with him — when she wasn't transcribing.

Pete was busy with fixing up a car he'd bought with his savings, a Toyota Land Cruiser like John's, plus putting quite a few hours of test flight on the Rebel.

They had the machine tools Ralph had given them set up and had made several tools to make working on the Rebel easier.

Pete had acquired a hundred rounds of ammo for the Sharps, and many evenings were spent reloading those he shot. He was becoming a skilled long range shooter, and targets with the bull full of holes adorned the shop wall. The Enfield was getting its share of use too, and the freezer was full of venison.

The Sunday afternoon ride up to the repeater station was pleasant. It was just John and Lois this trip. Pete could be heard off in the distance when he let off a round with the Sharps. Lois got their lunch out of her saddlebags and John spread the tarp.

The fried chicken was gone and the cup cakes were being devoured when Lois said casually, "I have some news for you."

John casually looked up and saw a mischievous grin on her face.

"Pete's going to have a brother — or sister. It's too early to tell which, but I found out Thursday."

She looked at John with her eyes twinkling.

At first John was stunned. He knew that it was frequent that recently wed couples produced children, but he'd just assumed they were too old for it to be likely. Then it hit him. She was waiting to see his reaction — they'd never talked of additions and she wasn't too sure he would want to start a new family at their ages.

He lit up with pleasure and rolled over to where she was reclining and folded her in his arms. "You sneaky little…" He kissed her roundly — a couple of times. "Why didn't you tell me Thursday night?"

She'd had a "routine" check-up at the doctor's.

"I wasn't too sure how you'd take it, what with our ages, and all…"

"You silly…" and the rest was lost in another happy kiss. "When?"

"New Years, maybe. At least that's what Dr. Schofield thinks."

*   *   *

Bill Hesseman was as good as his word. Bill had been Lois' mentor when she was working at the hospital in Vancouver, and when told she was getting married, had threatened to "…come out and look over this new husband."

He called and asked if he and his wife Dorothy could come to visit them for a few days in mid-August. That was fine; she knew John and Bill would hit it off. On the appointed day Bill arrived in his bright red Jeep Grand Cherokee.

Lois had never met Dorothy, and she turned out to be a delight, a perfect mate for the robust and vital Bill Hesseman. They were duly installed in a bed-room and dinner time approached. John and Lois were pleasantly surprised when Dorothy simply joined in with dinner preparations, setting the table and fixing the tea as though she'd lived here all her life. She and Lois were chattering a-mile-a-minute, and John and Bill were laughing between them-selves at how they had many mutual interests.

Pete finished reloading some shells in the basement and joined them in the living room, picking up on their enjoyment of the two women's laughing together.

"Got a question for you, John," Bill said, sipping his beer.

"A friend of mine is in a bind. He has a ranch and 8/900 head of buffalo in Saskatchewan. He's not in too good health, and he needs to sell off his herd. Do you know of anybody who might want to get into buffalo-raising?"

John thought a minute, then, "No. I don't know anything about raising them, nor do I know anyone around here that would."

Bill shrugged, and the conversation drifted to other things. Dinner was announced, and they headed for the dining room.

After supper the ladies were upstairs, Lois showing the house and Dorothy ooh-ing and aah-ing over layout, furniture, draperies, and the many things that make a house a home. Pete had a meeting of the EAA Chapter in Kamloops to attend but John begged off, due to their visitors. They were spending the evening in the shop, John showing Bill the Rebel, the machine tools, the latter now mounted and with appropriate benches around them.

The DOT inspector showed up the next day and went over the airplane and the log books, their records of test flights and related data. He was satisfied the requirements had been met, and signed the Rebel off in the Experimental Category. This meant that all test period restrictions were completed and the airplane could be flown as any other private airplane except that it could not be commercially operated.

"Does that mean that I can get a ride in it?" Bill asked as the inspector drove off.

"Sure does. If you're willing to risk your butt in a 'homemade' airplane, as the news people insist on calling them."

It was lunch time and they went in for the noonday feed. Dorothy had seen the plane, but was not too enthusiastic about Bill going up in it.

Lois chimed in with, "Well, for what it's worth, I've been up in it four times and thoroughly loved it. It's better than the Cessna we've been renting."

John went on to explain, "During the test period there have to be a set number of hours flown, doing certain maneuvers and within so many miles of its home airport, and no passengers are allowed. I declared her a member of the air-crew, and took her along a few times. Not absolutely legal, but unless somebody complains, there's nothing ever done about it."

Bill added, "That airplane has just been inspected by a DOT inspector, and is probably much safer than one of the many we've chartered over the years." That seemed to soothe Dorothy's fears, and the next morning was to be the day.

The Rebel, with two fully grown, husky men aboard, showed no effort as she grabbed air, climbing out at better than 900 feet a minute. John banked her toward the ridge and as they leveled off, still climbing, Bill was all eyes, looking over the range, the mountain, and the expanding scenery. He had been up in small planes many times, but this was something new. The others had been chartered, where he was merely a passenger sitting in a rear seat.

Here, he was sitting in the right hand seat with the instrument panel right in front of him and the entire panoply of windshield tailing off to the view from the side windows. He felt he could see everything — he could "see forever."

The mountain passed below them and Bonaparte Lake was approaching. John leveled off at 6500 feet and swung to fly directly over Bonaparte. The Lycoming was rumbling contentedly as the miles passed rapidly beneath them. John swung the nose southward and told Bill to take the stick in his right hand.

Bill did so, and soon realized that John had both his hands folded in his lap. John nodded at his feet, and took them off the rudder pedals. Bill quickly realized that he was now flying the plane, and that, after a few tentative movements of the stick and rudder pedals, it was very easy to control.

"Make a slight bank to the left — just press against the stick with your hand."

Bill did so, and the left wing dropped slightly and the airplane began to slowly turn to the left.

"Now, gently push to the right against the stick."

Bill did so, and the airplane righted itself and entered a shallow bank to the right. He was hooked!

*   *   *

Summer wore into Fall, and preparations for winter were in order. Caches of feed were located under the clumps of trees that dotted the landscape, and were covered with tarps to keep them dry until needed. This would save hauling during the worst of the snows, and provide the cattle with feed when they weren't able to haul it out every day.

John reached across Lois' desk and picked up the phone, dialing Bill Hesseman's home number. It was 8:05 in the evening, and he'd made up his mind.

"Bill? John Morgan here. Bill, would you please run that by me again about your friend with the buffalo?"

Chapter 10
Increasing the Population of Rebel Ranch

Bill Hesseman and the tall, stooped old man sat across the dining table from John and Lois. Dinner was over. Pete was in the office adjacent, at Lois' desk doing his homework, but with one ear tuned to the conversation. The dishes had been cleared away and it was time to talk buffalo.

Lawrence Boyd had been raising buffalo for twenty years in Saskatchewan, and had a sizable herd. He had fractured a couple of vertebrae several months ago and was forced to cut back on physical activity. This, on a cattle ranch, means quitting the daily work — ranch work is a physical job.

The generalities had been completed and they were getting down to specifics.

"It's very simple. I can't keep up with the work, and I can't afford to hire help. Not enough to keep things up the way they need to be. Buff don't need all the care reg'lar cattle do, but since me an' Louise are all by ourselves, an' we had girls instead o' boys, it don't leave us much choice. Our two girls married city boys. They're both fine boys, but neither of 'em would know a shovel from a pike. So, I gotta work out some deal so the herd will get the care they need, and I can settle down and more or less retire. That's where I'm at."

"How many head do you have?" John was interested in particulars.

"Little over a thousand. There was somethin' over 850, last I talked with Bill, but some have calved, so there's about a thousand, give or take a few. You have enough land to handle them, plus any increase for the next several years. Your grass looks good, and I have a buyer that'll go with the deal."

"Sounds pretty reasonable so far. Just how are they different than regular domestic cattle?"

"Well, they put on weight more slowly than beef cattle, but winters don't bother 'em. Where you have to take feed to snow-bound cattle, the buff will find his grass under the snow. They were feedin' themselves long before man came along."

The old man paused, thinking.

"Then, they don't need help droppin' calves, so that's somethin' else you don't have to worry about."

"Why the difference? Why are they so much more self-reliant?" John was getting more interested.

"Remember, these critters evolved on the American continent without man's assistance for some hundreds of thousands of years. Any animal in the herd that had difficulty in calvin' would simply die in childbirth, so to speak, and whatever was in their genes that caused the problem died with them. It was a simple case of survival of the fittest. Genetics."

"One thing I see that you'll have to do is to beef up your fences. Buffalo are easier to get along with, but they are a little less tame than domestic cattle. If they take a notion to go someplace, they're goin' to go, an' no barb wire fence is goin' to stop 'em.

"On the other hand, they're a lot less excitable than cows; they don't spook as easily, an' if they have all they want where they are, they're satisfied to stay in the one place."

136

"What do they need to have to keep satisfied?"

"Just like you. If you give them a comfortable place to stay with no annoyances, plenty of good food, some salt, and a willin' female within reach, they're in no hurry to move on."

Lois reddened with the reference and John chuckled at the old man's candor. Pete, in the other room, could hear all this, and had a hard time to keep from breaking out in a guffaw.

The whole thing sounded good to John so far, but the other end of the operation still had to be looked at.

"You mentioned a buyer. How does that work? Who buys buffalo?"

"There's a chain of restaurants down in the States that specialize in buffalo steaks an' roasts an' hamburgers. They've been growing pretty fast, and it looks like the popularity of buffalo meat is spreading. Then, there are a few markets that have tried selling buff meat, with good response. Their biggest problem is finding adequate sources. The demand is presently bigger than the supply. As far as I can tell there's not too many other ranchers that've gone into buffalo raisin', an' it's a seller's market at present. Since buffalo grow more slowly, it's probably goin' to stay that way for some while. The buyers work for the packin' houses, an' the sellin' is up to them. All you'll have to deal with is these buyers. There are two I've been dealing with, an' a third comin' up. So, there's some competition there."

"Are they any different to handle than regular cattle?" This was sounding better and better to John.

"Yes. Easier. I use a jeep or an ATV to move 'em. You can even walk among 'em, but not when they have young calves. They get annoyed then. Any other time all you have to do is get behind them with your vehicle and nudge 'em to start 'em movin' towards where you want 'em to go, an' they'll go wherever you want 'em to — new ground or corral or wherever.

"What I do is "educate" 'em when they're young; give 'em a nudge in the shins with the jeep or ATV a couple of times, an' after that they know what you want when the vehicle shows up and gets around behind 'em. But you never want to move 'em too fast or they'll get notions. Just drift 'em along easy-like, an' they'll go where you want. A man on horseback is OK, but I find a vehicle works better. They don't get excited too easy, but if they do, it'll take a real stout fence to stop 'em."

"How about shipping? Cattle trailers?" John was liking everything he heard.

"The buyers provide the transportation. But buffalo are easier to ship — once they get into the trailer and get settled down, they don't keep moving around like cows do. They also don't make the soupy mess cows do; they're much more placid about things."

"Well, now let's get down to cases," John said. "What do you have to have for me to get into the buffalo raising business"

"The sooner I get quit of the buff, the sooner I'll start feelin' better. I'm just gettin' too old to keep up. But I need some income. So, here's my offer." Larry Boyd leaned back in his chair and thought of how to phrase it.

"I have transportation and can ship my herd to you over the coming two months. It'll be best if you keep your cows separated from the buff. If you'll agree to pay me one half the cost of my shipment to you within the next year, and then 30 percent of your gross sales of buffalo for the following ten years, they're yours. This'll make us partners, instead of an outright sale. Like I said, I need an income, and this arrangement will do what I need."

"What kind of income have you been averaging over the past few years?"

This offer sounded like something that John's finances could handle, and if he went for the buffalo deal, he would have no need to keep the domestic cattle, and could easily sell them off.

Larry brought out a large envelope and spread contracts and sales papers on the table.

"Here's the present contract, which is transferable, and the past years' sales payments. You add 'em up, an' tell me if it sounds workable to you."

John pored over the sheets, passing them to Lois to look over. Some arithmetic told him that he could easily give Larry what he asked and still have a very good profit from the present contract, which extended for another four years.

"Mr. Boyd, I think we have a deal." Lois' nod had clinched his decision.

Larry stretched his hand across the table and John shook it in the age-old sign of agreement between men of honor.

* * *

On January 5 Alan John (AJ) Morgan was born. Pete had a brother! Lois, despite "biological clock" admonitions from her several neighbor friends, had come through in good spirits and health. It had been John who suggested his name, as he was smart enough to recognize that Lois's first husband's name was still dear to her, and her moist glowing eyes told him that he'd made the right choice. Pete spent hours playing with his tiny brother and watching in awe as AJ learned all about this brand new world about him.

He and John had made good time in getting a sturdy pipe framed fence around a part of the pasture before the buffalo began arriving. He had learned, through Bill Hesseman, of a carload of used oil-field pipe that was available cheap, and he and Pete had become expert welders by the end of the first week. With the coming of Spring the rest of the herd was arriving and the pair were kept busy building fence ahead of the increasing herd.

That didn't mean the Rebel was an orphan. John and Lois, with AJ, took two trips to Vancouver to show off AJ to Ralph and Evelyn by the advent of Summer.

"Dad," Pete had said after supper one night as the end of the school year approached, "I'm graduating in a few weeks, and I'm not sure I'm ready for college. But, I do want to get a degree. I like this ranch life, and, although I was playing with the idea of a Mechanical Engineering degree, I've been thinking that one in agriculture would be more suitable. What do you think?"

"I think you'd do well in either. But, I have to think that maybe Ag. Engineering might be better suited for you, if you plan to continue here as my partner."

"Partner?!" Pete exclaimed. "How do you figure that?" It was a whole new concept for him.

"Seems pretty natural to me. You've been my right arm ever since you arrived. And, I'm getting on in years, and figure I'll want to take some time now and then to go a few places, and who better to leave in charge than a partner?"

Lois had been hearing this, and winked at John. This was no news to her, as John had broached the idea to her a couple months before.

John continued, "Think about it, Pete. A farmer, or rancher, has to be a whole lot of engineers rolled into one; civil, to take care of grading and drainage, while allowing for adequate water storage for crops and cattle. Then he has to be a darn good mechanic to keep all the farm machinery in shape and make emergency repairs way out here, away from town. He has to be electrician enough to keep his well pump in working order without getting himself electrocuted, and he has to be carpenter enough to keep his buildings in repair, and make additions when needed."

"Then he has to be architect enough to plan any new buildings. You and Shirley have become pretty thick lately, and one of these days you may get some ideas about marriage. This is a big enough house, but the Chinese pictograph for trouble is two women under one roof. Do you get my meaning?"

Pete grinned sheepishly, nodding at John's wisdom. Lois smiled to herself. Although she would like to keep Pete with her, she too was wise enough to realize that newlyweds, whether Pete and Shirley, or another girl, wouldn't be comfortable living with their in-laws.

* * *

Summer vacation arrived — Glenn and Janet came to visit, hunt, fish and relax for a month. Glenn had brought along a Swedish Mauser rifle he'd picked up, a Model 96. It was in military trim, and looked like it had spent its life in an armory instead of the field. Pete was fascinated with the new piece, and Glenn wasted no time getting around to telling him some firearms history.

"The original Mausers that earned the name and fame were the Model of 1893, sometimes known as the 'Spanish Mauser', as they were used by the Spaniards in Cuba during the United States' war with Spain in 1898. With their staggered box magazine, sturdy bolt action, stronger and with greater range than the U.S. Krag, they were so superior to anything the Americans had that the U.S. promptly developed the Springfield of 1903, based on the Mauser design, but in .30 caliber. Until the outbreak of World War I, the U.S. paid the German government a five dollar royalty for each rifle made. The 1896 is a development of the 1893, made originally by Germany for Sweden and Norway, but soon made in Sweden at Husqvarna and at Carl Gustav's arsenal. That's where this one was made."

"What caliber is it?" Pete asked. "It looks smaller than my .30-06."

"It's in 6.5 X 55 millimeter. The bore is 6½ mm in diameter and the cartridge is 55 mm long. That's a common European way of denominating cartridge calibers."

"Is it any good for hunting?"

"You bet! They're noted for their accuracy in Europe. I have another, though, that I've rebarreled to .243 for a friend. The .243 is 6 mm on a .308 Winchester cartridge, necked down to .243. If you're going to mess around with shooting, you might as well get used to both metric and English measures."

"Where can you get ammo for it?" Pete was interested.

"Some gun shops carry it, but not too many. Anybody with one had better figure on hand-loading. Components can come from a dozen different mail-order houses."

"Handloading's no problem here. We've been loading .30-30 and .30-06 for some time," Pete responded, pride in his voice. "And .45-70," he added.

"Now who would you suppose taught John to load?" Glenn asked, tongue-in-cheek.

* * *

With the rifle on the workbench, Glenn removed the barrel bands and the upper wooden grip. On a trip into Kamloops they had picked up a nice sporter stock for a Class 2 Mauser at Libinatti's Gun Shop, along with a few boxes of 6.5 X 55 Swede Mauser ammo and some scope mounts. John had a good 3x-9x variable scope on the shelf, and the base and rings they had picked up would fit it to this action.

"That military 6.5 ammo Lib had was non-reloadable, unlike the .30-06 and .30-30. That's why we picked up these U.S.-made cases. They're Boxer primed, which means — if you're a reloader — that the primers can be easily removed and replaced. The European ammo with its Berdan primers can't be reloaded as easily." They had also bought reloading dies for the 6.5 Swede.

After removing the barrel bands and bedding screws, Glenn removed the barreled action from the stock, then removed the trigger-guard and magazine well from the bottom, laying the military stock aside. There was still preservative grease on much of the action, which Glenn removed with paper towels.

As he worked he rambled on, "First we cut the barrel to 24 inches — that 29 inch barrel is a mite too long to be handy in the field. Fine for long-range sniping, but cumbersome."

Glenn stripped the bolt, trigger assembly and military sight from the action and barrel, measuring 24 inches from the action toward the muzzle. Taking a silver pencil, he marked the 24 inch location on the barrel. "That's where we cut," he commented.

Next he threaded the barrel through the spindle of the lathe, placing aluminum strips under the three lathe chuck jaws as he tightened them on the barrel. He placed a magnetic based dial indicator on the compound of the lathe, moving the carriage so as to place the indicator foot against the barrel. Turning the lathe by hand, he watched the indicator needle. It flickered from 0 to a little over 15 thousandths.

"Too much run-out. Better we use a steady-rest." Glenn released the chuck jaws and ran the barrel further through the chuck, until the action was against the left end of the spindle, before re-tightening the jaws.

He then took a dead center from the rack and placed it in the tailstock, running it up gently but snugly into the muzzle of the rifle.

"That'll hold it on center with the bore while we adjust the steady-rest," Glenn said, reaching for the latter item as he spoke.

He set the steady-rest in position on the lathe bed, about three inches to the left of where they planned to cut the barrel off, and snugged down the mounting clamp.

He swung the hinged top portion of the steady-rest over and fastened the latch-bolt.

After gently snugging the three fingers of the steady-rest against the barrel, and further checking that all was as it should be, he locked each finger solidly in position, and then gave each roller a generous dose of way oil.

Now, when he turned the lathe chuck over by hand, there was no movement of the indicator needle, showing that all was running true.

Finally, he fitted a narrow cut-off tool into the toolholder and positioned it roughly at the mark made earlier with his silver pencil.

As he finished these preparations, Glenn explained to Pete, "Setting the muzzle on a tailstock center, and then setting the steady rest fingers to the barrel OD, makes sure the bore is concentric, so when we crown it, we won't have any runout there. The crown is critical to accuracy."

Glenn moved the tool until it lined up with the silver pencil mark, and locked the carriage travel, and then looked at Pete.

"You ever use this lathe?"

"Sure. John taught me while we were building the plane. We had lots of things we needed to make, small fittings and special stuff we thought would work on the bird, but that didn't come with the kit."

"Okay, Pete. Cut the barrel off."

Pete stepped up to the lathe, turned it on and cut into the barrel while squirting cutting oil onto the tool from a pump can. As the tool neared the bore, he backed off the dead center so the cut-off end of the barrel wouldn't jam, and soon the end of the barrel fell off.

"Now what do you do?" Glenn asked, challengingly.

"I'll crown it. Can't hit anything with a rough cut-off like this."

He rummaged around in a drawer under the bench and came up with a tool ground to a shape well suited to machining the inside of something small and tubular. Fitting it into the tool holder, he brought it up near the new muzzle end of the barrel. Turning on the lathe, he eased the tool against the inside edge of the bore, cutting gently, until the exit area of the muzzle was rounded, with a true inner edge against the rifling just showing. He rounded the outer edge slightly, then shut off the lathe.

After removing the steady-rest and putting it back in its place on the rack, he loosened the chuck jaws and withdrew the barreled action, handing it silently to Glenn.

Glenn inspected the finished cut, then grinned at Pete. "Looks like I taught my son pretty well, an' he taught you the same way. You'll do. By the way, this is your rifle. How about we glass-bed it into that stock tomorrow?"

*   *   *

One evening a couple of weeks later there was a new development at Rebel Ranch...

"Dad, Mom, C'mere. We've got something to show you," Pete called up the stairs.

"Okay. Be down in a minute," floated down the stairs. Shortly John followed Lois down the stairs and into the living room. "Whatcha been up to?" John said, looking at the handsome couple standing, waiting for them.

"This," Pete said, as he took Shirley's left hand and held it out so they could see the sparkling ring on her third finger.

"We're engaged. We're to be married when I finish college. Yesterday I received notice that I was accepted, and Shirley said she'd have no trouble waiting for me."

The tall, auburn-haired young lady that Lois and John had fallen in love with over the past couple of years sparkled as she smiled.

"Dad, I have you to thank. If you hadn't taken me and made a real man out of me, I'd never have met such a wonderful young woman as this. And Mom, if you hadn't had the courage to let me come and live with John, I don't know what I'd have become, but nothing like I am now. I called Grandpa," — he'd taken to calling Glenn "Grandpa" since their visit weeks ago — "and asked if I could live with him and Janet while I'm going to school, and he said they'd be glad to have me. So, I guess I have a row to hoe for the next four years."

Pete hadn't finished his speech before Lois had stepped forward and thrown her arms around Shirley in welcome. John's eyes were swimming as he said, "When I first saw you I asked myself, 'What's this the cat dragged in?' Since then, you've made me the proudest man alive. I kind of expected you'd do something like this — hoped it — prayed for it. Congratulations, Son!"

END